Mystery on the Menu

Nancy peeked through the doorway of the kitchen. She saw Regis, the chef, beating some eggs with a wire whisk. "Are you all right?" Nancy asked, wondering if he'd recovered from the poisoning attempt.

"I'm fine, thank you," the chef replied.

"I heard that Officer Reed isn't pressing charges. I can't believe it, can you?" Nancy asked, stepping into the room.

"What can I say?" Regis cried. "The police can't seem to recognize a simple case of attempted murder. It was Alicia, I know it. And mark my words, she will try it again. She is a desperate person who will stop at nothing to—"

Suddenly, Nancy heard a strange whistling noise in the air. A split second later, a ten-inch knife whizzed right between Nancy and Regis!

Nancy Drew
Mystery Stories

Available from MINSTREL Books

NANCY DREW MYSTERY STORIES®

117

NANCY DREW®

MYSTERY ON THE MENU

CAROLYN KEENE

A
MINSTREL®
BOOK

PUBLISHED BY POCKET BOOKS

New York   London   Toronto   Sydney   Tokyo   Singapore

This book is a work of fiction. Names, characters, places, and incidents either are products of the author's imagination or are used fictitiously. Any resemblance to actual events or locales or persons, living or dead, is entirely coincidental.

A MINSTREL PAPERBACK *ORIGINAL*

 A Minstrel Book published by
POCKET BOOKS, a division of Simon & Schuster Inc.
1230 Avenue of the Americas, New York, NY 10020

Copyright © 1993 by Simon & Schuster Inc.

Produced by Mega-Books of New York, Inc.

ISBN: 0-671-79303-9

First Minstrel Books printing February 1994

10 9 8 7 6 5 4 3 2

NANCY DREW, NANCY DREW MYSTERY STORIES, A MINSTREL BOOK and colophon are registered trademarks of Simon & Schuster Inc.

Cover art by Aleta Jenks

Printed in the U.S.A.

Contents

Contents

MYSTERY ON THE MENU

1

George's Surprise

"You owe me twenty dollars, Bess," George Fayne said gleefully, waving an envelope in the air. "I'll take cash or a check."

Bess Marvin looked up at her cousin with a bored expression on her face. She and Nancy Drew, the cousins' best friend, were sitting in the living room of the Drew house reading magazines. George had just arrived and was standing in the doorway, her cheeks pink from the cold.

"What are you rambling on about, George?" Bess asked, turning a page of *Creative Cuisine*. Her blue eyes lit up. "Oh, Nan, look at this dessert— Chocolate Macadamia Nut Pie. Couldn't you go for a piece right about now?"

Eighteen-year-old Nancy leaned over and studied the photograph, pushing back a lock of her reddish blond hair as she did so. "That looks yummy, all right."

George shook off her red ski parka and joined the other girls on the living room couch. "Can you two stop jabbering for one second and listen to something really exciting?"

"Okay," Bess said, flipping her magazine shut. "*Why* do I owe you twenty dollars?"

"Desserts," George said, her brown eyes sparkling. "The Valentine's Day dessert contest, remember? I won!" She handed Bess the envelope she'd been holding. "This letter just came from the culinary institute that ran the contest."

"What are you guys talking about?" Nancy asked.

Bess scanned the letter quickly, twirling a lock of her long straw blond hair with one finger. "I can't believe it," she moaned. "Here I set out to make the easiest twenty dollars of my life, and it backfires on me!"

George ran a hand through her short, curly dark hair and grinned at Nancy. "You see, Bess read about this contest in one of her food magazines, and she dared me to enter it. It was being run by the Wolfe Culinary Institute—"

"The Wolfe Culinary Institute in Putney Grove, New York?" Nancy broke in. "That cooking school is really famous. You entered one of its contests?"

George nodded proudly. "They asked for an

2

original dessert recipe with a Valentine's Day theme, and three winners would get a week of dessert-making classes. Bess said I couldn't boil water, much less come up with a decent recipe. I guess she was wrong!"

"Way to go, George," Nancy said, patting her friend on the back. "So what was this award-winning recipe?"

"Raspberry Chiffon Cake," George said, smacking her lips. "It's based on something my grandmother used to make, except I've adapted it for health-conscious people. It's low calorie and low fat."

"And low taste, probably," Bess grumbled, fishing a twenty-dollar bill out of her purse and handing it to her cousin.

"Sore loser." George grinned, stuffing the money into her jeans pocket. "For your information, my cake tastes great."

"So when do your classes start?" Nancy asked George.

"February seventh," George replied. "The finale is a big party on Valentine's Day, featuring the three winning recipes." She sat up suddenly. "Hey, guys. I have a terrific idea. Why don't you come with me?"

Nancy looked surprised. "What do you mean, come with you? We didn't enter the contest."

"I know that," George said. "But from what I understand, the dessert-making classes are open to

3

the public. The other two winners and I just happen to get them for free. Come on—it'll be great! Seven whole days of baking cakes, pies, cookies . . ."

Her blue eyes twinkling, Nancy turned to Bess. "What do you think?"

But Bess was already up and heading for the door. "Excuse me, guys, but I have some major shopping to do," she said over her shoulder. "I'll need a chef's hat, an apron, and maybe some very baggy sweaters, just in case I gain a pound or two."

"This place is a cooking school?" George exclaimed. The three girls had just driven up to the front door of the Wolfe Culinary Institute and were getting out of Nancy's blue Mustang. "It looks more like a millionaire's mansion."

Before them stood a huge, ornate Gothic structure, much like a medieval castle. It had dozens of turrets and chimneys, and its dark gray walls were made of rough-cut stone. Gargoyles—eerie-looking animal statues—jutted out from the eaves.

"It *is* a millionaire's mansion," a voice called out.

The girls turned to see a short, plump woman coming around the side of the house. She had spiky red hair and dark blue eyes and appeared to be in her early forties.

"That is, it used to be a millionaire's house, about four decades ago," the woman continued, unzipping her black down jacket and pulling off her black leather gloves. "Since then it's been a museum, a corporate headquarters, and a private boys' school. I bought it when I started the institute."

"Then you must be Sophie Wolfe, the owner," Nancy said. She introduced herself, then George and Bess. "We're here for the dessert-making classes."

Sophie smiled. "I'm so happy you've come. And, George, it's especially thrilling to meet the creator of the fabulous Raspberry Chiffon Cake. Your recipe was a big hit with the contest judges."

"Thank you," George said, blushing.

"Where should we take our bags?" Nancy asked Sophie.

"Right upstairs," Sophie replied, leading them through the heavy oak front door. "We've converted what used to be the servants' quarters into dorm rooms. I think you'll be comfortable there."

True to her prediction, the girls fell in love with their room immediately. It was airy and artfully decorated, with dark mahogany paneling, purple velvet curtains, and an ornate Oriental rug. Still-life paintings of food adorned the walls.

"I'll leave you to get settled," Sophie said cheerfully. "At two o'clock, we're all gathering in the lobby. I'm giving the students a tour of the place. We'll be seeing the grounds as well as the house, so dress warmly."

Promptly at two o'clock, the girls made their way down the winding stone staircase to the first floor.

There were more than a dozen people in the lobby already. The girls spotted Sophie talking to a petite middle-aged woman.

Sophie looked up when she saw Nancy and her friends. "Nancy, Bess, George—let me introduce you to everyone."

She started with the middle-aged woman, whose name was Lila Barnstable. Lila had a silvery blond pageboy and deep brown eyes.

"How do you do?" Lila said to the girls. "Are you all training to be professional chefs?"

"No, we're just here for fun," Nancy explained. "How about you?"

Lila smiled. "Same with me. I just love taking classes. You know, cooking, ceramics, Spanish, bridge, archery . . ."

Bess's eyes widened. "You've taken archery lessons?"

"Oh, sure—it sharpens the mind," Lila joked.

Sophie then introduced the girls to George's fellow contest winners. The first one, Paul White, was a handsome young guy with wavy brown hair, green eyes, and high cheekbones. He mumbled a quick hello, then resumed his conversation with two other young guys, both blond. The third contest winner was a young woman dressed in a patchwork dress and lace-up boots. She was a waitress from New York City named Teddy Angell.

"Teddy?" George repeated, puzzled.

The woman flipped back a strand of long, curly auburn hair and rolled her eyes. "It's short for Theodosia. I mean, what kind of parents name their kid Theodosia?" She studied George. "What about you? What does 'George' stand for?"

"Georgia," George replied, smiling with understanding.

Next Sophie introduced the girls to Gloria Chen, an attractive woman in her late thirties. She had waist-length black hair and a tall, slim build.

"Pleased to meet you," Gloria said, shaking hands with all three girls. She adjusted her copper-colored glasses on her nose and focused her amber eyes on Nancy. "You look familiar. Are you with the press?" She added eagerly, "Maybe you're a book reviewer?"

"Nancy's a famous detective," Bess piped up. "She's solved dozens of mysteries back in our hometown, River Heights, and lots of other places. You've probably seen her picture in the papers."

Nancy frowned briefly at Bess. She didn't like advertising the fact that she was an investigator, even when she wasn't on a case.

Nancy then turned to Gloria with a friendly smile. "I'm here strictly for pleasure, though. How about you?"

But Gloria seemed to have been caught off guard. She turned a shade paler and was silent for a moment before she replied: "I'm a cookbook writer. I'm here to brush up on my dessert-making skills."

Nancy studied Gloria curiously. What had made her change her manner? The fact that Nancy was a detective? Or was she just disappointed to find that Nancy wasn't a book reviewer who might help her career?

"A cookbook writer!" Bess was saying excitedly. "We've got scads of cookbooks at home. Maybe some of them are yours."

Gloria's eyes gleamed. "Oh, I'm sure of it. I've got seven best-sellers under my belt. How about *Gloria's Kitchen*—do you have that one? Or *Gloria's Favorite Breakfasts and Brunches?*"

Bess shook her head apologetically. "No, they don't ring a bell. But I'll take another look when I get home," she added.

Sophie interrupted just then to complete the introductions. Nancy, Bess, and George met the two blond guys who'd been speaking to Paul White —Jamie and Taylor Morris, brothers who co-owned a café in Minneapolis—and the remaining six students, who belonged to an amateur cooking club in New Jersey.

Sophie clapped her hands loudly, and the crowd fell silent. "Welcome to the Wolfe Culinary Institute, everybody," she said. "I'm going to take you on a tour of the house and the grounds. Then, at four o'clock, you've got your first class with Regis

8

Brady. Now, let's start outside and work our way in."

Sophie headed out the door and everybody followed. Once outside, she paused at the edge of the U-shaped driveway.

Nancy looked out at the wide, snow-covered lawn. To the north and south, it was bordered by vast woods; to the west, it led to craggy gray cliffs overlooking the Hudson River.

"We have a hundred acres of land," Sophie explained. "Over there, by the woods, you can see where our cross-country skiing trail begins. You're welcome to try it out while you're here."

She led the group around the corner of the big house. "Now, there"—she pointed—"is our greenhouse. And the wooden case next to it holds our beehive."

"Did you say beehive?" Bess said, grimacing. "You mean with real bees? The kind that sting?"

Sophie grinned. "They won't sting you if you don't bother them. In fact, they hibernate during the winter, so as long as you don't perform batting practice with their hive, they'll leave you alone."

She added, "We keep bees for the honey. One of my most important rules here at the school is to work with the freshest ingredients. If possible, I think, you should obtain it yourself. It makes you a better chef when you know where the food comes from. We also have a chicken coop, so we can have

9

fresh eggs. And behind the greenhouse there's the vegetable garden, which our year-round students cultivate."

Lila Barnstable spoke up. "So you have year-round students?"

"We offer degrees here, just like a university, except they're all in the culinary arts," Sophie replied. "Our regular students are on their holiday break now, so they're not around. We take advantage of their holidays to conduct special events like this one. It's a way to let a lot of other people learn the fun of gourmet cooking."

"How old is the institute?" Taylor Morris asked.

"We'll be five years old this fall," Sophie explained. "That's relatively young compared to the Leblanc School in New York City and the Metzger Center for Culinary Arts in Baltimore. They've been around for years! But, I'm proud to say, we've already got the highest enrollment of any cooking school in the country, including the Leblanc and the Metzger. And we've won many prizes from the top food magazines and organizations."

By three-thirty the group had seen most of the grounds as well as the first floor of the house. There were two wings off the lobby: the north wing, which contained ten fully equipped classrooms, and the south wing, which contained offices, an auditorium, a living room, a rec room, and a dining hall.

At the end of the tour Sophie guided the students

10

to the large main kitchen, which was adjacent to the dining hall. Nancy had never seen such a state-of-the-art kitchen before. It had gleaming stainless steel counters and enormous ovens with complicated valves attached to them.

Four men and two women were moving around the kitchen, busily preparing dinner. Sophie explained to the group that they were the staff chefs, who would be cooking all the students' meals.

"Smells yummy," Bess whispered to Nancy.

Suddenly a loud voice broke in. "I insist on a green salad with my meal. This is absolutely *ridiculous.*"

Nancy's ears perked up. In the corner of the kitchen, a very large dark-haired man was barking at one of the chefs.

"But the fruit salad will complement the rest of the dinner so nicely," the chef protested.

The large man huffed. "Whoever created this menu is obviously a fool. A fruit salad with Beef Bourguignon? Ha! Don't make me laugh!" Then he stormed dramatically out of the kitchen.

"Who was that?" Nancy whispered to Sophie, who was standing right next to her.

Sophie smiled weakly. "He's Regis Brady, one of the two guest instructors I've hired for the dessert classes. He's a world-famous pastry chef from New York City. He has a restaurant there called Brady's." She sighed. "I know he comes across as a little difficult, but he's really quite a genius in a kitchen. You'll see."

"We have a class with him at four, right?" Nancy said.

"Right. He'll be teaching a four o'clock class every day." Sophie nodded. "The other guest instructor, Alicia Jones, will teach the morning classes. She's fabulous, too. She owns a restaurant in New Orleans called the Honeysuckle Café, and she specializes in Southern desserts. Wait until you taste her Mississippi Mud Pie—sheer heaven!"

Sophie paused to glance at her watch. "Speaking of four o'clock, it's almost that time now." She clapped her hands to get the group's attention. "Ladies and gentlemen, your first class will be in fifteen minutes in room eleven—with Regis Brady."

After dropping their coats off in their room, Nancy, Bess, and George headed for room 11, which was the fourth room past the lobby in the north wing. The other students were already there, milling around outside the door.

"I wonder what we'll be cooking—" George began. But just then she was interrupted by loud voices coming from a room down the hallway.

"You have no right to speak to me this way!" a woman's voice exclaimed.

Nancy, George, and Bess exchanged puzzled looks. Nancy noticed that the other students had fallen silent and were listening, too.

12

"You talk to me about rights?" a man said in reply. Nancy recognized Regis Brady's voice. "Ha! You have no right to be at this institute. We both know that you're an impostor, Alicia. And if you know what's good for you, you will pack your bags and leave the premises immediately!"

2

First Course: Danger

Nancy frowned. "Alicia" must be Alicia Jones, the other guest instructor, she thought. But what did Regis mean about her being an impostor?

"Listen here, Regis Brady—" Alicia began angrily.

"I've said all there is to say on the subject," Regis interrupted. "Now, if you will excuse me, I have a class to teach."

A second later Regis came striding down the hallway. With him were two small corgi dogs, one red and one brown, with very short white legs and no tails. They ran in circles around him, panting excitedly.

"What are you all staring at?" Regis snapped at

Nancy and the other students, who were still clustered around the doorway.

"Excuse me, but those dogs . . ." Paul White spoke up hesitantly.

Regis raised one eyebrow. "What about them?"

"I'm allergic to them," Paul explained. "Not severely allergic, but even still—"

"My dogs accompany me to all my classes," Regis interrupted. "If your allergy is nothing serious, then you may sit in the back, and Peaches and Truffles will stay up front. I trust that will be a satisfactory arrangement?"

Paul sneezed, then nodded weakly.

The students followed Regis and his dogs into room 11. Like the main kitchen, it was large and full of gleaming stainless steel and oversize, high-tech equipment. In the middle of the room were two long worktables, each with a dozen sinks and individual counter spaces. Beside each sink, a cutting board, assorted knives, and a bowl of fruit had been set out.

Bess quickly assumed a place at one of the long tables and rolled up the sleeves of her pink sweater. She then reached in her purse, pulled out a brand-new chef's apron and hat, and put them on.

"I'm ready," she announced cheerfully, reaching up to center the tall white hat on her blond head. "What are we making first, Mr. Brady? Pecan pie? Strawberry shortcake?"

Regis stared, amazed at Bess's outfit, then said, "We are not making *anything* today, young lady. A great chef must first learn basic cutlery skills. Today we will chop, slice, and carve."

"Oh," Bess said, frowning in disappointment.

After everyone was settled, Regis strode to a small worktable at the head of the classroom. Peaches and Truffles followed, curled up at his feet, and immediately fell asleep.

Regis reached into a wooden box on his worktable. "This is my personal knife collection, which I will now share with you," he said solemnly. "All great chefs always carry their own knives."

He lifted out a shiny ten-inch blade and turned it over in his hand. "This one is used for mincing, slicing, and dicing," he said. "Watch closely while I demonstrate."

Regis selected an apple from a bowl of fruit and began working on it. The blade made a swift staccato noise on the cutting board.

Within five seconds, the apple had been reduced to a neat pile of cubes, with the core, seeds, and stem discarded to the side. "Voilà," Regis murmured. "And now, ladies and gentlemen, you will do the same. Pick up your knives and your apples."

For the next half hour, the room was filled with the sounds of chopping. The class went through dozens of apples, pears, bananas, kiwifruits, and strawberries.

Regis circled around and studied everyone's

progress. "Very good," he said to Teddy Angell. "You have done this before."

Gloria Chen, Nancy, and George got similar praise, but Bess was criticized for her slowness. "You have only cut up two pieces of fruit in all this time?" Regis asked.

"I sampled some of it," Bess admitted sheepishly. "You know, to make sure that I, um, was doing this right."

Regis scowled at her, then moved on to Lila. "Point your blade down, toward the board," he told her. "Then rock it up and down, very fast."

Next Regis spent some time with the six cooking club people from New Jersey. Finally, he made his way to the three young men—Jamie, Taylor, and Paul—who were at the back of the room.

"Good," Regis said to the two blond brothers. "But you—" He turned to Paul, his voice growing shrill. "What are you doing there? That is a knife, not a chain saw! You are making a mess!"

Paul blushed deeply as the other students turned to look at him. On his cutting board lay a gooey red lump—the remains of a strawberry—and a pear hacked in ragged halves.

Regis grabbed Paul's knife from his hand and deftly began slicing the pear. "*This* is how you do it," he said loudly. "It is very simple."

"Poor Paul," Bess murmured to Nancy and George. "I mean, it's not like we're doing this for a grade."

After the students had finished their chopping lesson, Regis returned to his own table. He reached inside the wooden box once more and pulled out a four-inch paring knife.

"I will now teach you how to carve fruits into beautiful shapes," he announced. "In a future class, we will use this skill for decorating cakes and tortes. Now watch closely while I turn this plain little kiwifruit into a masterpiece."

In almost no time at all, Regis had transformed the fuzzy green fruit into a dozen delicate daisies. He then turned a strawberry into a rose and an apple into a long chain of half-moons.

"Now I want you all to try your hands at this," he instructed. "Take your paring knives and pick out some fruit. I will not dictate to you what shapes you should create. You are the artists. Use your imaginations! Be inspired!"

Regis began another tour of the room, peering intently over the students' shoulders as they worked. Once again, when he got to Paul he lost his temper.

"What is this?" Regis cried out, pointing to three uneven banana slices. "Can you do *nothing?* Here, give me that knife."

At six o'clock, when class was over, Paul was the first to head for the door. As he passed the girls, Bess reached out and put a hand on his arm.

"I wouldn't pay much attention to that man if I were you," she said gently. "I think he's kind of an ogre."

Paul frowned at her, then hurried away.

Bess turned to Nancy and George. "Was it something I said?" she asked.

George shrugged. "Maybe he's just shy."

While waiting for dinner to be announced, Nancy and the girls sat in the living room in front of the fireplace. The only other people in the room were Teddy and the Morris brothers, who were discussing the art on the walls.

Bess leaned back into the plush velvet couch and stretched her toes toward the roaring fire. She plucked a curried shrimp ball from a plate of hors d'oeuvres on her lap. "Mmm," she murmured. "Is this the life, or what?"

Just then, a tall, slim man crossed in front of them and knelt down before the fireplace. Reaching for an iron poker, he began stirring up the fire.

"Hi, there," Bess called out, popping the shrimp ball into her mouth.

The man turned, adjusting his tortoise-shell glasses as he did so. He had a long, pale, freckle-covered face and light, almost platinum blond hair. Nancy guessed that he was in his mid-forties.

"Can I help you?" he asked coolly.

19

Nancy, Bess, and George exchanged puzzled glances. "Um, no," Bess said. "We're students here. I'm Bess Marvin, and these are my friends George Fayne and Nancy Drew."

"I am Baird Goldensen, the administrative vice president of the institute," the man said.

"So you work for Sophie," George spoke up.

"I work *with* Sophie, yes," Baird replied crisply.

At that moment a gong rang.

"Dinner," Baird said, and started toward the hallway. "If you will excuse me."

"Why don't any of the men here have any manners?" Bess exclaimed when Baird had walked away.

"It's probably something in the water," Nancy joked.

The girls stood up and strolled into the large, elegantly furnished dining hall. The other twelve students were already there, as were Baird Goldensen and Regis Brady. Sophie introduced Alicia Jones, the other teacher, to the students.

Alicia Jones was a tall, attractive woman in her forties with shoulder-length black hair and high cheekbones. She wore a jewel-colored silk caftan. A deep blue scarf around her neck complemented her dark brown skin. Nancy wondered what this pleasant-looking woman could possibly have done to make Regis Brady so angry.

"I'm happy to be here," Alicia said to the group

after Sophie's introduction. "And I'm looking forward to teaching you all about chocolate tomorrow morning."

"Chocolate?" Bess echoed. "I'll be there bright and early!" Everyone burst into laughter.

There were ten small tables in the dining hall, with four seats at each table. Nancy, Bess, and George decided to sit with Teddy.

"Nice-looking grub," Teddy remarked as they started on their first course.

"I've never seen such a pretty fruit salad," Bess marveled. "Or such a weird one. I mean, what *is* this?" She speared a smooth orange-colored wedge with her fork.

"I think that's a mango," Nancy said. "There's also some papaya in here, and starfruit."

At the next table Regis was sitting with Sophie and Baird. "Ah," Nancy heard Regis say in a smug voice. "This is the proper first course for this meal."

Nancy glanced over her shoulder. Regis was eating his specially ordered green salad.

"You two will be sorry you didn't insist on one of these yourselves," Regis told his companions. "Sophie, you *must* talk to that so-called chef of yours. He is an amateur, an inexperienced . . . an inexperienced . . ."

Regis hesitated, then cleared his throat. "I'm sorry, I'm suddenly feeling . . ."

21

He put his fork down with a clatter. His face was growing flushed.

"Do you need some water, Regis?" Sophie asked, worried.

In reply, Regis groaned and clutched his stomach. Then he doubled over and tumbled helplessly out of his chair.

3

Flowers Can Be Fatal

"Regis!" Sophie screamed.

Nancy had already leaped from her chair and rushed to the fallen man's side. She knelt down on the floor and studied his half-open eyes.

Sophie leaned over anxiously. "Should someone perform the Heimlich maneuver on him?"

"No—I don't think he's choking," Nancy replied. "He reached for his stomach, not his throat."

"Ohhhhh," Regis moaned.

George and Bess had joined Nancy. The others in the room hovered in a semicircle near the table.

"Can we help, Nan?" George asked.

"I think he's been poisoned," Nancy announced gravely. "Someone should call an ambulance right away. And get the police, too."

"Poisoned!" Sophie exclaimed. "Poisoned! Oh, no, how can that possibly—" She stopped and shook her head briskly. "I'm sorry, this is no time to get hysterical. George, Bess, the closest phone is in my office, right across the hall."

Within ten minutes two young medics arrived, followed by a police officer. The medics began working on Regis immediately.

"Who's in charge here?" barked the gray-haired officer.

"I am," Sophie said, stepping forward to read the name on his badge. "I'm Sophie Wolfe, the head of the institute." She then told Officer Reed what had happened. "This young lady here, Ms. Drew, thinks that Mr. Brady was poisoned," she finished.

Officer Reed looked at Nancy skeptically. "Oh, you do? And what makes you think that?" he asked.

"I simply observed his symptoms," Nancy replied. She pointed at Regis's salad. "This is what he was eating when he collapsed."

Officer Reed glanced at the plate. "What is that, anyway?"

"It's our standard green salad," Sophie explained. "It contains Bibb lettuce, watercress, chrysanthemums, and nasturtiums."

"Chrysanthemums and nasturtiums!" Officer Reed exclaimed. "The last I heard, those are flowers."

"*Edible* flowers," Sophie corrected him. "We use

24

a variety of them in our cooking here. We grow them in the greenhouse."

Officer Reed frowned. "No wonder the poor man keeled over. Flowers belong in a vase, not in a— hey there, what do you think you're doing?"

Paul White had stepped in front of the rest of the crowd and was studying Regis's salad intently. He jumped in surprise when Officer Reed addressed him.

"I—um—I couldn't help noticing something," Paul mumbled.

"What's that? Speak up, young man. What did you notice?" Officer Reed said sharply.

"There are some strange-looking flowers in here," Paul said. "They don't look like either chrysanthemums or nasturtiums."

Officer Reed bent down and peered closely at the salad. When Nancy leaned over the salad, too, he frowned at her. "Do you mind?" he said.

Nancy pointed at several ripped-up white petals. "You're right, Paul," she said. "At first I thought they were nasturtiums. But now they look to me like lily of the valley, which are incredibly poisonous— even the stems and leaves."

"Lily of the valley!" Sophie cried. "How did they end up in Regis's salad?"

"Do you grow them in your greenhouse?" Nancy asked her.

"Well, yes," Sophie admitted. "We grow a number of nonedible flowers—we use them for centerpieces and decorations. But they're clearly labeled. Our chefs would never make that kind of mistake—they know exactly which flowers are edible and which ones aren't."

Officer Reed looked thoughtful, then walked over to the medics, who were placing Regis on a stretcher. Reed instructed them to take a sample of Regis's salad with them.

After they had gone, Officer Reed glanced around at the anxious faces in the dining hall. "For the moment, I want you all to stay in this room," he told the group. "I don't want any of you touching anything, including your own food. I'm going to take a look around, then I want to talk to all of you. Understand?" He nodded at Sophie. "You, Ms. Wolfe, please show me to the greenhouse."

"Of course," Sophie said.

As Officer Reed and Sophie left the room, Nancy leaned over to Bess and George and said, "I'm going to ask if they'll let me tag along." She slipped out of the dining hall and followed Officer Reed and Sophie down the hallway.

"The greenhouse is right over here," Sophie was saying, pointing to a door. "There's another entrance from the outside, but—"

Just then Officer Reed spotted Nancy. "I thought I told you to stay in the dining hall," he said. "This is police business, young lady."

Nancy looked levelly at him, then at Sophie. "I'm

a private detective," she said. "If it's all right with both of you, I'd like to come along. I might be able to offer some help."

"It's fine with me," Sophie replied immediately. "This is a very serious situation—we need all the brainpower we can get."

Officer Reed frowned at Nancy. "Well, you did identify the lily of the valley—*if* that's what those flowers are. I won't be convinced until the hospital lab checks it out." His frown deepened. "All right, I guess you can come along. Just don't get in my way, understand?"

"Absolutely," Nancy assured him.

When Sophie opened the door to the greenhouse, a wave of warm, humid air greeted them. Inside was a jumble of colorful vegetables, herbs, and exotic-looking plants.

Sophie led them down one of the aisles. "This is where most of our edible and inedible flowers are," she explained. "And here are the lily-of-the-valley plants."

Nancy bent down and studied the small flowers. One plant in particular caught her interest. "Look at this, Officer Reed," she pointed out. "This plant has one bare stem. Someone has ripped all the blossoms off it."

Officer Reed nodded. "I see what you mean. But couldn't it just be unhealthy? Maybe the blossoms fell off."

"That's not very likely." Sophie shook her head.

"The rest of the plant is healthy—the leaves are in perfect condition."

Nancy squinted. "From what I can tell, too, it looks as though whoever ripped the blossoms off did it recently. The nicks on the stem are still fresh and green, not dried up or brown."

"I can't believe it," Sophie said. "Who on earth would do such a thing?"

"Wait a second," Officer Reed interrupted. "Look what's growing right next to them." He waved a hand at several white funnel-shaped flowers. "Nasturtiums."

"Are you saying that whoever picked the nasturtiums for Regis Brady's salad accidentally picked the lily of the valley, too?" Nancy asked. "I don't see how. The nasturtiums are much bigger—no one could possibly confuse the two."

Officer Reed shrugged. "I'm not saying that's what happened. I'm just saying let's not assume we have a case of attempted murder on our hands until we get all the facts." He turned to Sophie. "Now, Ms. Wolfe, I want you to fill me in on everyone here. Then I want to talk to them all, starting with the cook who put the salad together."

Sophie gave him a rundown on the institute's current inhabitants, then told him about Louis Drake, the chef. She explained about Regis's argument with Louis over the salad choice. "Louis creates all the menus for the meals, then oversees their execution," Sophie added. "I don't know if he made Regis's salad personally or had an assistant do it, but either way, I can't imagine that anyone in my kitchen would mistake lily of the valley for nasturtiums!"

As they headed for the main kitchen, Nancy wondered if she should mention to Officer Reed the argument between Regis and Alicia. After a second's thought, she decided against it. She had overheard just a piece of the conversation, and without knowing more, she didn't feel comfortable putting Alicia on the spot with the police.

In the kitchen the six staff chefs and three assistants were standing around anxiously. Officer Reed took Louis Drake aside and started questioning him immediately. Then Nancy heard the chef burst out angrily: "I would *never* mistake an inedible flower for an edible one!"

"Did you pick the flowers for the salad yourself, Mr. Drake?" Nancy spoke up.

Louis turned to her, startled. "No, not at all," he said more calmly. "It is my recipe, of course, but my assistant Gerard did all the work. He picked the flowers and greens and made the salad." He indicated a young, freckle-faced guy of eighteen or so. "Gerard, come here."

Officer Reed spent the next few minutes grilling Gerard. The assistant chef insisted that he had not confused the two flowers.

"When was Mr. Brady's green salad taken to the dining room?" Nancy asked Gerard.

"We set out all the salads at about six forty-five," Gerard said nervously. "That's how we always do it with salads. That way, the people can start right in when they sit down at the table."

Nancy nodded. "Did you notice anyone else in the dining hall when you were taking the salads out there? Or anytime after that?"

Gerard shook his head. "There was nobody there while we were taking the salads out," he recalled. "And after that we were all real busy in the kitchen. Anybody could have come in and out of the dining hall without us noticing."

"Okay, that's all for now." Officer Reed dismissed Gerard and Louis. "I want to speak to some of the other chefs and assistants in here, then move on to the dining hall."

An hour later Officer Reed had learned nothing new, except that the first diners in the hall had been the six cooking club members from New Jersey, at five till seven. According to them, no one had gone anywhere near Regis's salad between then and the time Regis showed up, at around seven.

When Officer Reed finally left at ten o'clock, everyone was exhausted. By the time Nancy joined Bess and George at their table, most of the diners were heading up to bed. Everyone had lost their appetites.

"Where's Sophie?" George asked.

"She and Baird Goldensen went to the hospital to check on Regis," Nancy replied.

"Isn't this awful?" Bess murmured. "It's our first day here, and there's a killer on the loose!"

Nancy rubbed her forehead wearily. "I wouldn't go that far, Bess. Officer Reed thinks the poisoning may have been accidental."

"What do you think, Nan?" George asked. "I mean, you got all the same facts he did."

Nancy glanced around. The only people left in the dining hall were the Morris brothers, who were across the room.

"I don't think it was an accident," Nancy told her friends. She told them about what she had seen in the greenhouse. "I think someone meant to poison Regis Brady—someone who happens to know that lily of the valley is incredibly toxic," she concluded.

"But who?" George said.

Nancy shrugged. "It's too early to tell. I'm wondering about Alicia because of that argument she and Regis were having this afternoon." She lowered her voice. "But now that I think about it, there's also Paul. Regis raked him over the coals today, and Paul looked pretty upset about it."

"Paul?" Bess shook her head. "No way. He's too cute to be a murderer. Besides, he's the one who pointed out those flowers in Regis's salad."

"That's true," Nancy admitted. "Of course, he could have done that to throw us all off."

"One thing's for sure, Nan," George declared. "I

31

think you've gotten yourself involved in another mystery."

Before breakfast the next morning, Sophie came to the girls' room and told them that Regis would soon be well.

"It *was* lily of the valley in his salad," she explained. "Fortunately, he only got a little bit of it into his system. He recovered very quickly after they treated him at the hospital. They may even release him this morning."

"That's wonderful news," Nancy said. "Of course, there's still the question of how the flowers got into his food."

"I know," Sophie said gravely. "Officer Reed is eager to question Regis about it." She paused and shook her head. "This may sound very odd, but I'm hoping it turns out Gerard or Louis or someone put those flowers in Regis's salad accidentally. It would be terrible if one of my employees had made that kind of mistake, but—"

"—it's better than thinking that one of us students might be a murderer," Nancy finished.

A few minutes later Sophie and the three girls headed down to breakfast. When they reached the lobby, however, a commotion awaited them.

Regis was standing just inside the doorway, clutching a cane in his right hand. He was surrounded by a small crowd of people, including Alicia, Baird, Paul, Lila, and Gloria. His face was pale, and there were dark circles under his eyes, but his voice still boomed arrogantly.

"A grave injustice has been done!" he shouted, banging his cane against the stone floor.

"Regis!" Sophie cried out. "When did you get back? Why didn't you call us? Are you all right?"

"I am fine, Sophie—except for the fact that Alicia Jones is standing here rather than eating gruel in a jail cell," Regis declared.

He focused his small black eyes on Alicia, who stared at him with her mouth open. "Yes, that's right, Alicia," Regis snarled dramatically. "You're the one who tried to poison me last night. And there's no way you're going to convince me otherwise!"

4

Too Many Cooks

Everyone in the lobby stared at Alicia.

"Have you lost your mind, Regis?" Alicia exclaimed. "I know we're not exactly best friends, but this is absurd."

Sophie turned to Regis. "I don't understand, Regis. Do you have some sort of proof to back up what you're saying?"

"Proof?" Regis repeated scornfully. "What proof do I need? This woman is threatened by my presence here at the institute, and she made a desperate attempt to remove me. Need I say more?"

Alicia shook her head in anger. "I will not stand here listening to this slander," she said. "I'm going to get some breakfast." She turned on her heels and walked away, flipping her blue silk scarf over her shoulder as she did so.

"She is running away! A true sign of guilt, if I ever saw one!" Regis called after her.

"Regis, please," Sophie begged. "Let's go into my office and discuss this—in private."

She led him away, and the small crowd began to break up.

"Come on, guys," Nancy whispered to George and Bess. "I want to talk to Alicia. Let's see if we can get her alone."

"Do you think she did it?" Bess whispered back.

"Not necessarily, but something's going on between her and Regis, and I want to know what it is," Nancy replied.

The girls found Alicia carrying her plate of food toward an unoccupied table in the dining hall. Teddy and the six cooking club members were seated at two other tables.

After the girls had introduced themselves and sat down, Nancy said, "We wanted to talk to you about what just happened. You must be upset."

Alicia picked at her scrambled eggs and sighed heavily. "That man is just too much," she said.

"We overheard the two of you arguing yesterday," Nancy told her gently. "Do you think that's why Regis thinks you poisoned him?"

"That was no argument," Alicia said coolly. "Regis marched into my classroom and ordered me to leave the institute. It was an unwarranted, one-sided attack, pure and simple."

"But why?" George asked. "Why is he so eager to get rid of you?"

Alicia was silent for a moment. Finally, she said, "Sophie has decided to add a full-time dessert instructor to her staff. She's going to offer the job to either Regis or me. We're both extremely interested, and Sophie's having a hard time making up her mind. Having us here this week, watching us work with the students, is going to help her choose."

"But don't you and Regis have restaurants to run?" George asked, puzzled.

"We both have managers who could run the restaurants in our absence," Alicia replied. "And speaking for myself, I would love a new challenge at this point in my career."

She took a sip of coffee. "There's a very simple explanation for Regis's behavior," she added. "You see, he has half a dozen degrees from the best culinary institutes in the world. I, on the other hand, never studied formally—that's not my style. I grew up in a family of wonderful cooks, especially my mother and my grandmother. I work with their recipes, as well as other traditional recipes passed on through generations of women in my community."

"So Regis feels that you're not in his league?" Nancy said.

"Exactly," Alicia replied, her brown eyes flashing. "Despite the fact that I own a successful restaurant and I've won a number of awards, Regis considers me an amateur. So when he found out that Sophie was trying to choose between him and me, he was furious. He thinks it's an insult."

"Wow," Bess exclaimed. "I guess Regis wants you out of here so he doesn't have to risk coming in second place behind you."

"Exactly," Alicia said. "But he'd never admit to it."

Nancy frowned. "But what about his accusations this morning? Does he really think you should be in jail?"

Alicia nodded. "Absolutely. He'll tell the police, Sophie, or anyone else who'll listen, that I'll resort to desperate measures to get the job—even murder."

"Do the police know about the two of you being in competition for this job?" Nancy asked her.

"I told them all about it this morning," the older woman replied. "Regis called them from the hospital and told them to arrest me immediately. I got a visit from Officer Reed at dawn—well, it seemed like dawn, anyway." She grinned. "I'm not much of a morning person."

Alicia glanced at her watch, then dabbed at her lips with her napkin. "Listen, ladies, it's been nice unloading all my frustrations on you, but I'd better get ready for class."

After Alicia left, the girls filled their own plates with breakfast and resumed discussing the case.

"Alicia's story sounds convincing, doesn't it?" Nancy said. "I can see Regis Brady resenting Alicia and trying to bully her into leaving the institute." She bit into a cranberry muffin. "Yum."

"Go on," George prompted. "I know there's more. I can tell by that gleam in your eyes."

"There *is* more," Nancy said, chuckling. "Even if Alicia is right about Regis, that doesn't automatically rule her out as a suspect. She has plenty of motives for wanting him out of commission. The job, for one thing. Or maybe she just got sick of his insults and decided to get even."

Just then Sophie came rushing up to their table. "I'm sorry to interrupt," she said, "but I just got a call from Officer Reed. He's going to rule the poisoning an accident."

"What!" George exclaimed.

"He thinks that Louis Drake's assistant Gerard mixed the flowers up by mistake," Sophie explained.

"But Gerard said he didn't," Nancy said.

"Gerard is young and inexperienced," Sophie replied. "He may *think* he didn't mix the flowers up, but who knows?"

"What about Alicia?" Nancy persisted. "What do the police think of Regis's accusations?"

"Officer Reed thinks Regis is just being melodramatic," Sophie said. "I must admit, I have to agree with him there. Alicia is no murderer.

"Frankly, I'm relieved," she continued. "I just hope that's the end of it. The institute isn't used to all this excitement."

Nancy was silent. Deep down, some instinct told her that the excitement wasn't over yet—not by a long shot.

Nancy dipped a finger into her bowl of white chocolate mousse and tasted it. A little more vanilla, she decided.

"You're all doing beautifully," Alicia announced to the students. "So beautifully, in fact, that I'm going to move on to stage two."

Nancy's eyes wandered in Paul's direction as she measured out a half teaspoon of vanilla. She realized that Alicia was being very generous with her praise of the class. Once again Paul was struggling with the lesson—his mousse was a lumpy mess. But unlike Regis, Alicia was patient with Paul. More than once she had gone to his side and talked him through the steps.

"You're all going to like stage two," Alicia said, moving to the front of the classroom. She held up a small bag full of balloons. "We're going to blow these up and use them to serve the mousse."

"You mean we're going to stick balloons on top, like decorations?" Lila Barnstable asked. "We did something like that once at my bridge club luncheon."

Alicia smiled. "No. We're going to use these balloons to make bowls for the mousse. Here, let's get started."

Alicia proceeded to show the students how to dip the blown-up balloons in melted dark chocolate. "Just the bottoms of the balloons," she told them. "Then put the balloons, chocolate side down, on some parchment paper to dry."

A short while later, Alicia took one of the balloons and separated it carefully from its now hardened chocolate coating. The result was a delicate chocolate bowl.

"Now you have an elegant way to serve your mousse," Alicia said. "You put the mousse inside the bowl and add some sliced strawberries or slivers of orange rind on top for color."

"An edible bowl—cool!" Teddy Angell called out approvingly.

At the end of class Alicia told the students that the mousse would be served at lunch. "I've made extra, so there'll be plenty," she said.

As Nancy washed her hands, she spotted Paul heading out the door. All morning, she'd had a nagging feeling that Officer Reed was missing something. She decided to do a little more sleuthing.

She caught up to Paul in the corridor. "Hi," she

said cheerfully, falling into step beside him. "I've never made mousse before, have you?"

Paul frowned at her. "No. Excuse me, I'm in kind of a hurry."

"So did you hear what the police are saying about Regis Brady?" Nancy persisted.

She thought she caught a flicker of interest in his green eyes. "What?" he said.

"They're ruling the poisoning an accident," she said in a low voice.

"An accident?" Paul repeated.

Nancy told him about the flower mix-up.

"Hmm," Paul murmured. "It doesn't say much for this school, then, does it? I mean, if one of the employees can make that kind of a mistake, how can we feel safe eating the meals here?"

"But what if it wasn't a mistake?" Nancy asked. She paused, choosing her words carefully. Now that she was finally getting this cold, quiet guy to talk, she didn't want to blow it. "What if it was attempted murder?"

"Murder?" Paul echoed. "But who'd want to murder that old goat?"

"Exactly my point," Nancy said eagerly. "Regis isn't making very many friends here. Look at the way he was yelling at Louis Drake, the chef, about his salad. And his argument with Alicia. And the way he treated you in class."

"Me?" Paul said, looking surprised. "He doesn't bother me."

41

Nancy fixed her gaze on him. "Are you sure about that? He was pretty hard on you yesterday."

Paul stopped in his tracks and stared at her suspiciously. "Are you suggesting that maybe *I* tried to poison him because he got on my case in class? Give me a break. I'm not crazy enough to murder someone, just because he criticized my chopping technique."

Nancy stood silently, fidgeting. She had to admit that he had a point.

"Take my advice," Paul continued. "Stick to cooking and leave the detective work to the police." Then he turned and walked away.

Later that afternoon Nancy left George, Bess, Teddy, and Jamie Morris playing Monopoly in the rec room. She had learned from Sophie at lunchtime that Regis planned to go ahead with his schedule despite his illness. She wanted to arrive early for his class so she could talk to him alone.

Nancy peeked quietly through the doorway of room 11. She saw Regis beating some eggs with a wire whisk. He still looked pale and seemed weak —he had to lean against the table as he worked.

"Are you all right?" Nancy asked.

Regis looked up, startled. His two corgis, who had been napping at his feet, woke up and began barking.

"Truffles, Peaches, be quiet," Regis ordered,

then fixed his dark eyes on Nancy. "I'm fine, thank you. But class isn't for another twenty minutes."

"I just wanted to see how you were feeling," Nancy said, moving into the room. She crinkled her brow, trying to look concerned. "I heard that Officer Reed isn't pressing charges. I can't believe it, can you?"

That hit the right nerve. Regis flushed red with anger.

"What can I say?" he cried, throwing his hands up. The whisk he was holding showered the air with drops of egg. "The police can't seem to recognize a simple case of attempted murder!"

"I know you think Alicia Jones was responsible," Nancy said. "But—"

"Ms. Drew," Regis interrupted haughtily. "I don't *think* Alicia was responsible. I *know* it."

"Of course," Nancy said with a smile. "But can you think of anyone else here who might have had a motive?"

Regis shrugged. "Except for Alicia and Sophie and Baird, and some of the chefs in the kitchen, I have never met these people before in my life." He looked down at the eggs and began whisking them violently. "It was Alicia. I know it. And mark my words, she will try it again. She is a desperate person who will stop at nothing to—"

Suddenly, Nancy heard a strange whistling noise in the air. A split second later a ten-inch knife whizzed right by Regis's head!

43

5

A Strange Encounter

As the knife clattered against the wall right behind his head, Regis dove under the table.

"We're under attack!" he cried out. "Peaches, Truffles, seek cover!"

Nancy crouched low to the ground and spun around. The knife had come flying from the direction of the doorway, but no one was standing there.

"Don't touch that knife," she said firmly to Regis. Then she stood up, tiptoed to the door, and poked her head outside. There was no sign of the assailant.

Thinking quickly, Nancy decided to head for the lobby. The assailant was likely to have escaped in that direction, where there were several exits.

Just then she noticed something on the floor of

the hallway. She bent down to pick it up. It was a blue silk scarf.

Alicia had been wearing a similar scarf earlier, Nancy recalled. And she was sure it hadn't been lying on the floor a few minutes ago.

Did that mean Alicia was the assailant?

Putting her thoughts on hold for the moment, Nancy continued on to the lobby. To her disappointment, it was empty.

Just then a door swung open and Baird Goldensen strolled in, his face buried in a newspaper.

"Twenty down," he muttered to himself. "Three-letter word. Flightless Australian bird."

"The answer is emu," Nancy said quickly. Baird looked up, startled. "Mr. Goldensen, did you happen to see anyone come running through here just now?" she asked.

Baird frowned at her. "No, I didn't. Why?"

Nancy explained what had happened.

"I'm afraid I can't help," Baird said, looking concerned. "I've been sitting in the living room for the last half hour doing this crossword puzzle. And as you can see, we keep the door between the two areas closed." He sighed. "I'd better go call the police right away."

After a few more minutes of fruitless exploring, Nancy rushed back to room 11 to check on Regis. He was nowhere to be seen.

"Mr. Brady?" she called out, worried.

Then she caught sight of his feet sticking out from under the table, along with his dogs' white paws. She stifled a chuckle.

"It's safe to come out now, Mr. Brady," Nancy reassured him. "The police are on their way."

Regis popped his head out, looked around suspiciously, then got to his feet. Truffles and Peaches wriggled out after him, whimpering softly.

"Are you all right?" Nancy asked him.

"I'm extremely angry," Regis huffed. "If the police had only done their job and arrested Alicia Jones this morning, this never would have happened."

Nancy looked down at the silk scarf in her hand. Was Regis right? she wondered.

"Regis!"

Sophie burst into the room. "Baird told me what happened," she said breathlessly. Her anxious blue eyes swept over him. "Are you hurt?"

"I'm perfectly fine," Regis replied coolly. "In fact, I am rather glad this macabre little culinary incident occurred. Now maybe the police will listen to me when I tell them that—"

"Excuse me," Nancy interrupted, walking toward the door. "I'll be back in a few minutes."

Stepping into the corridor, Nancy ran smack into Baird, who was hovering near the door. "I'm sorry," she apologized, startled. "Listen, do you know where I can find Ms. Jones?"

Baird reached up to straighten his glasses. "I believe I saw her going into the living room," he replied crisply. "Sophie asked me to inform the students that Regis's class would be postponed indefinitely. I came to let her know that I've taken care of it. Is she in room eleven?"

"Yes," Nancy said, then continued on her way.

In the living room, she found Alicia sitting in a chair by the window, leafing through a cooking magazine. On the table beside her was a steaming mug of tea. There was no one else around.

"Ms. Jones?" Nancy said. She noted that Alicia was not wearing a scarf around her neck.

Alicia looked up and smiled. "Oh, hello, Nancy. Please—call me Alicia."

Nancy sat down in a nearby chair and held out the blue scarf. "Is this yours, by any chance?"

Alicia leaned forward and peered at it. "Why, yes," she said, sounding surprised. "Where did you find it? I've been searching for it all afternoon. I took it off during class so I wouldn't get chocolate mousse on it, then it disappeared."

Nancy was silent. Was Alicia telling the truth? she wondered. If so, that meant that Regis's assailant had stolen her scarf and planted it in the corridor to make her look guilty.

Alicia's voice cut into her thoughts. "Will you please tell me what this is all about?"

"Of course," Nancy said. She told Alicia about

the knife attack on Regis and how she'd found the silk scarf right outside the doorway.

"The police will be here soon, if they're not here already," Nancy continued. "We should let them know about the scarf. Will you come with me?"

"Certainly," Alicia said, standing up. "But I'm not looking forward to it. This is exactly the sort of 'evidence' Regis has been waiting for. When he hears about it, he'll demand I be dragged away in handcuffs right then and there."

By the time Nancy and Alicia got to room 11, the police had already arrived. Nancy noticed several officers searching the corridor for clues.

Sophie was inside the room, wringing her hands. When she spotted Nancy and Alicia, she managed a weak smile and approached them.

Alicia glanced around. "Where's Regis? He's all right, isn't he?"

"I convinced him to go up to his room," Sophie explained.

"Ms. Drew." A gray head poked up from beneath Regis's worktable. It was Officer Reed. When he stood up, Nancy saw that he was holding the assailant's knife in a plastic bag.

"I hope you get some fingerprints off that," Nancy told him.

"We'll do our best," Officer Reed said. "Now, young lady, I'll need to get a statement from you. I understand you were here when it happened."

Nancy described in detail what had happened in the last hour, including her discovery of the blue scarf. "The scarf wasn't there when I came to see Mr. Brady at three-forty," she said.

"It's my scarf." Alicia spoke up immediately. Officer Reed raised his eyebrows. "But I didn't throw that knife," she added quickly. She then repeated everything she'd told Nancy in the living room.

"Where were you after three-forty?" Officer Reed asked her.

Alicia frowned, trying to remember. "Around three-forty I was in the main kitchen boiling water for tea. Louis Drake was there—he can vouch for me. But between then and . . . oh, four o'clock or so, I went up to my room to get a magazine."

"Did you see anybody in the lobby or on the stairs when you went up to your room?" Nancy asked.

"I don't think so," Alicia replied.

Officer Reed cleared his throat. "Ms. Drew, Ms. Jones, I'll want you both available for further questioning, if necessary," he said gruffly. Then he turned to Sophie. "I'm going to roam around and talk to some of the others."

"By all means," Sophie said. When he had gone, she turned to Nancy. "Could you come to my office for a moment?"

"Sure," Nancy replied.

Sophie and Nancy bid Alicia goodbye and headed for the office, which was in the south wing.

Once they were seated in her office, Sophie fixed her troubled eyes on Nancy. "I really need your help," she said gravely.

"What kind of help?" Nancy asked.

"As much as I hate to believe it, somebody seems to be after Regis," Sophie admitted. "I want the person caught before he really gets hurt."

"Why don't you just ask him to leave?" Nancy suggested. "That would get him out of immediate danger."

Sophie shook her head. "I already asked him, before the police arrived. He refused. He said, and I quote, 'I will not allow a second-rate dessert chef and criminal to scare me away.'"

Sophie leaned forward. "I know the police are doing everything they can," she went on. "But I'm afraid for Regis's safety. And I'm also afraid of what will happen to this school's reputation." She paused, then said, "I'd like you to conduct your own investigation—a low-key one that won't attract any publicity. You'd have an edge over the police because you're an insider here."

"I'd be happy to take on the case," Nancy said. She didn't mention that she already had been sleuthing around. "George and Bess can help out, too. They've worked with me in the past."

"Wonderful," Sophie said with a sigh.

"I'd like to keep it a secret that you've asked me to investigate," Nancy said. "Some of the people already know that I'm a detective, but if they don't think I'm working on this case, it will make things easier for me."

"Of course," Sophie agreed.

"Oh, and before I go I'd like to get all the files you have on your employees, plus Regis and Alicia," Nancy said. "And the copies of the students' application forms."

While Sophie was gathering the material together, Nancy said, "By the way, what's at the end of the north wing, past the classrooms?"

"Not much," Sophie replied, handing Nancy a stack of folders. "There's a small section of the hallway we never renovated—it's still in the old style, with stone walls and floors. The only room there is an office we use for storage—you know, a place to keep files, that sort of thing. And at the very end of the hallway, you'll find a door leading down to our wine cellar."

After thanking her for the folders, Nancy headed upstairs to her room. When she got there, she found Bess and George sitting on one of the beds playing gin rummy.

"Hi, Nan," George called out. "Class was canceled for some reason, so we've been amusing ourselves. What have you been up to?"

Nancy dumped the files on a table and plopped

down in an oversized red armchair. "We've got a job to do, guys," she announced. She proceeded to fill them in on what had been happening.

"You were right there when the knife came flying in?" Bess gasped. "Weren't you terrified?"

Nancy's eyes flashed. "The assailant was interested in Regis, not me. And he or she had great aim. The knife missed him only by inches."

"Do you believe what Alicia told you about the scarf?" George asked Nancy.

"I don't know," Nancy replied, frowning. "Sophie said this morning that Alicia's not a murderer, but I'm not entirely convinced."

"So where do we begin, Nan?" Bess asked.

Nancy nodded toward the files on the table. "I want you two to start going through those files Sophie gave me. They're full of information on the staff and the students here. Check the details of everyone's background, and keep your eyes open for a link between Regis and any of the others."

"Like if someone used to work at his restaurant in New York?" Bess offered.

"Right," Nancy said. "Regis claims he doesn't know anyone here but Sophie, Baird, Alicia, and some of the chefs—but who knows?" She stood up, went to the closet, and pulled out a red sweater. "And while you two are doing that, I'm going downstairs to poke around in the north wing."

George looked puzzled. "You mean look for clues? Haven't the police already done that?"

Nancy slipped the sweater over her black T-shirt and leggings. "Probably, but I want to get a sense of the area. Regis's assailant may have been hiding in one of the other classrooms before sneaking up on us."

After promising to meet back in the room before dinner, Nancy headed downstairs.

Nancy spent the next half hour going into each of the classrooms, including room 11. Finding nothing of interest, she continued down the hallway. True to Sophie's words, the last part of it was completely unrenovated, with the walls and floor made of craggy gray stone. The area was drafty and badly lit, with one bare light bulb halfway along. She wished she'd thought to bring her flashlight with her.

Down at the end of the hallway she spotted what she assumed to be the door to the wine cellar. Off to the right was another door—probably to the old storage office Sophie had mentioned.

Then, suddenly, Nancy realized she had company.

A figure crouched in a shadowy corner next to the cellar door. From the back, Nancy couldn't see who it was, but she thought that the person was examining something on the ground.

She felt the muscles in her neck tense. Could this be Regis's assailant?

Nancy backed up a few steps—but her footsteps made some noise. The figure started, then stood up and turned around. In the dim light, Nancy could make out the silvery blond pageboy. It was Lila Barnstable.

Lila smiled nervously and brushed a lock of hair from her forehead. "Oh, hello, Nancy," she murmured. "Funny meeting you here."

"I was just about to say the same thing," Nancy replied. She glanced around. "It's kind of a lonely spot to be wandering around, isn't it?"

"Yes, it is," Lila agreed, her smile wavering. "I was just . . . I was just studying the detail on this stone floor. I recently took a class in the history of architecture, and I'm absolutely fascinated by this old house."

"Really?" Nancy said politely. But she could see by the anxious look on the woman's face that she was not quite telling the truth.

Nancy decided to find out for sure. "Isn't this cornice wonderful?" she said brightly, pointing to the stone molding along the bottom of the wall. "You can tell the architect really spent a lot of time designing it."

"Oh, yes," Lila agreed quickly. "I noticed that right away. It's quite lovely."

Nancy tried to curb her excitement at Lila's reply. Anyone who knew anything about architecture would realize that the cornice was the molding along the top of a wall, not the bottom. Nancy had deliberately pointed at the wrong thing, and Lila hadn't noticed her mistake. She was clearly not an architecture buff. What was her real reason for being down here?

After a brief silence, Lila said, "Maybe I should be heading upstairs."

"I'll go with you," Nancy said with a smile. "I was going to take a look at the wine cellar, but I guess I'll save that for another time."

Nancy and Lila parted company in the front hall, and Nancy went back to her room. George and Bess were sitting on the floor, surrounded by files. Nancy told them about her encounter with Lila.

"There's something fishy about the woman," Nancy concluded.

"What do you suppose she's up to?" Bess asked.

Nancy shrugged. "I'm not sure. But I intend to find out." She glanced at the files. "How are you guys doing with these? Did you find anything?"

"Not really," Bess replied.

"Let me help," Nancy offered, picking up a file and plopping down on the floor with her two friends.

"Interesting," Nancy said a while later. "I'm looking at Paul White's application form for the dessert contest. There's almost nothing on it."

Bess threw Nancy a scornful look. "Are you picking on poor Paul again?"

"I think it's weird that he has a post office box in New York City for an address and no phone number," Nancy replied. "And under 'Occupation' it just says 'self-employed.'"

"Self-employed what?" George asked.

Nancy frowned. "It doesn't say. And there's no emergency contact listed."

"Hmm," George mused. "That is kind of weird."

At dinner Nancy and the girls decided to split up. George sat with Paul and Alicia, who were together at one table, and Bess joined Regis and Baird. Nancy ended up with Lila and Gloria Chen.

"So you're a cookbook writer?" Lila said to Gloria as the three of them started on the soup course. "That must be interesting."

Nancy brought a spoonful of pumpkin soup to her lips. She watched the silver-haired woman make small talk with Gloria. Was it her imagination, or was Lila nervous?

"I love my work," Gloria answered in a solemn reply to Lila's comment. "Of course, I might not love it as much if I weren't so successful at it. Fame is nothing to sneeze at."

"You must go to a lot of restaurants, Gloria," Nancy said smoothly.

Gloria dabbed at her lips with a white linen napkin. "Oh, yes," she said. "I go out to eat quite often wherever I am. In Los Angeles, Chicago, Paris, New York—"

"New York," Nancy repeated. "Maybe you've been to Regis Brady's restaurant, then? I think Sophie mentioned it—Brady's, right?"

"Right." Gloria glanced around, then leaned forward toward Nancy and Lila. Her copper-colored glasses slid down her nose ever so slightly. "Actually, I haven't been there. But I know people in the business, and they tell me it's overrated."

Nancy turned to Lila. "Have you been there?"

"Oh, no," Lila replied, looking startled. "My husband and I live in Connecticut, but we don't get down to the city much. We're sort of homebodies."

"Connecticut?" Gloria said enthusiastically. "Have you tried Edward's Bistro in West Hartford? It's a wonderful place, although I could teach that chef a thing or two about roasting pheasant."

"So what do you two think about the weird things that have been happening here?" Nancy asked.

"Do you think it's the work of an outsider?" Gloria asked, her amber eyes glittering. "Or do you think it's one of us?"

"One of us?" Lila repeated, shuddering. "What an awful thought."

Nancy watched Lila closely. What was this woman hiding? Was she just pretending to be frightened by the thought of Regis's assailant being in their midst? Was she the assailant—or did she know who it was?

* * *

57

Hours later Nancy lay in bed, deep in thought. Bess and George were sound asleep, but Nancy was having trouble drifting off. Her mind dwelled on the case and all its complications. Somebody was after Regis, but who? Paul? Alicia? Lila? Or another person altogether?

Nancy sat up suddenly and swung her slender legs over the edge of the bed. She had to go back down to the cellar door, to the spot where she'd found Lila. The woman had been looking at—or for—something. Maybe Nancy could figure out what.

Nancy dressed, grabbed a flashlight, and headed downstairs. The mansion was still and dark; everyone was asleep.

As Nancy made her way down the north wing hallway, past all the closed classroom doors, she felt a shiver of apprehension.

Snap out of it, Drew, she told herself sternly. You're used to poking around old houses after hours.

In the unrenovated section of the hallway, the air was cold and damp. Digging her free hand deep into the pocket of her sweater, Nancy swung her flashlight to the right, at the door of the old office, then straight ahead, at the wine cellar door. She moved toward the latter.

Nancy crouched down and studied the wall and floor adjacent to the cellar door. She ran her fingers over the craggy gray stone. What had Lila found so interesting? she mused.

Just then she heard a soft noise behind her. Mice? she wondered briefly.

Then—*crack!*—a sharp pain exploded in the back of Nancy's head!

6

Up in Smoke

Nancy sank to her knees, trying to fight the blackness that threatened to envelop her. Stay awake, she told herself firmly. Stay awake.

She could hear footsteps receding into the distance behind her. She tried to turn around, to get a glimpse of her escaping assailant, but the motion was too painful.

"Ouch," she moaned, reaching behind to touch her head gingerly. A small lump was forming at the bottom of her skull, just above her neck.

Nancy realized then that she had dropped her flashlight. She pawed at the floor around her.

The flashlight lay next to her feet. "Bingo," she said, picking it up.

Shining the flashlight at the floor and walls surrounding her, Nancy wanted nothing more than to find a clue. But she knew she had to get upstairs and into bed, to sleep off the dizziness.

Tomorrow, she told herself.

Gathering her strength, Nancy tried to stand up. The effort was difficult, but she managed to get upright after a while. Then she took slow, careful steps down the hall toward the lobby.

After what seemed like an eternity, she reached her room. Bess and George were still sound asleep. Without bothering to undress, Nancy staggered to her bed and collapsed onto it.

After breakfast the next morning, Nancy returned to the north wing corridor, accompanied by Bess.

"I can't believe you came down here by yourself in the dead of night, Nan," Bess said, shuddering. "You could have been lying on this creepy old floor for hours, and nobody would have missed you."

Nancy clicked off her flashlight. "Nothing in the corridor," she announced. "Why don't we try that storage office? My attacker could have been hiding there before sneaking up on me."

She opened the door, flipped on a light switch, and walked in. The small, dank room looked as though it hadn't been cleaned in years. In the center stood an oak desk with two swivel chairs.

61

Against one wall was a row of beige metal file cabinets. Stacks of cardboard boxes lined the opposite wall.

Nancy bent down to peer at one of the boxes. She pulled out a thick file of yellowed papers and began leafing through it. "Old articles on the institute," she said, scanning them. "It says here that this house used to be called Fairgate Mansion, after its owner. Maybe Fairgate was the rich guy Sophie was talking about."

"What rich guy?" Bess asked.

"Sophie said that this house used to be a millionaire's mansion forty years ago," Nancy reminded Bess.

Nancy picked up several more files and looked through them. "Here's an article about one of Sophie's competitors. The Leblanc School in New York City—I think she mentioned it."

"Hmm," Bess murmured. She had picked up several files herself and was poring over them. "Wow," she exclaimed. "Look at these, Nan—recipes! Here's one for Ham, Cheese, and Onion Pie, and Rhubarb-Apple Cobbler . . ."

Nancy leaned over to look. Her friend was holding some folders marked "Recipes—Wolfe Culinary Institute Staff and Guest Chefs." Inside were pieces of paper covered with scribbles in different handwriting.

"Interesting," Nancy said. "These are original recipes by chefs who've worked or taught here."

They continued searching the office for any clues to Nancy's attacker. After a while they decided to give up.

"Let me get this straight," Bess said to Nancy as they closed the office door and started walking toward the lobby. "You think someone was hiding in there before sneaking up on you?"

"Maybe," Nancy said thoughtfully. "One possible explanation is that my attacker was in this area doing something—"

"What?" Bess prompted.

Nancy shrugged. "I have no idea. Anyway, the person was doing something, heard me coming, hid in the office, then hit me on the head. Or else he or she was somewhere else in the house, spotted me heading this way, and then followed me."

"But why?"

"To scare me off the case," Nancy answered.

"Ugh," Bess said, shivering.

"The question is, how did the person know I was *on* the case?" Nancy mused. "And what does Lila have to do with all this, if anything? She seemed so nervous when I ran into her yesterday—like I'd caught her doing something."

They had reached the lobby. Nancy hesitated for a moment, then pointed to the door to the south wing. "Let's go see if everyone's still having breakfast," she said. "I want to find out where all our suspects were last night around eleven. You take Alicia, and I'll take Lila and Paul."

"Whoever whacked you on the head isn't going to admit being down here last night," Bess pointed out.

Nancy shrugged. "You never know."

Their questioning was fairly fruitless, however. Lila and Alicia both claimed to have been asleep at eleven. Paul told Nancy that he'd been playing cards between ten and midnight with the Morris brothers, who backed him up.

"Now what?" Bess asked Nancy as they headed up to their room to get ready for Alicia's morning class. "If Paul, Lila, and Alicia didn't hit you over the head, who did?"

"I agree that Paul's innocent," Nancy said. "He's got two guys who can account for his whereabouts. But Lila and Alicia can't prove they were in their rooms at eleven. They could have been lying."

"That's true," Bess agreed.

"Or it could have been somebody else altogether," Nancy said.

Bess sighed. "This is getting complicated."

They found George in their room, lying on the floor doing some stretching exercises. "How did you guys make out?" she asked.

Nancy plopped down on her bed and brought George up-to-date on the morning's events.

"So what's your next plan of action?" George asked Nancy.

"I'm going to call Officer Reed and see if he got any fingerprints off that knife," Nancy said. "And maybe after Alicia's class I'll try to talk to Regis again. He could tell us something that might be useful to us."

"Yesterday we learned how to create chocolate bowls using balloons," Alicia said to the class. "Today we're going to continue with the theme of visually appealing food presentations. But first, can anyone tell me what this is?" She held up an oval-shaped fruit with spotted dark-green skin.

"It's a mango, of course," Gloria Chen said in a bored tone of voice. "Everybody knows that."

"There was mango in our fruit salads," Bess piped up. "You know, the ones we had the night . . ." She hesitated, blushing. Nancy could see that Bess was kicking herself for bringing up the poisoning incident, since Alicia was a prime suspect.

Alicia looked at Bess strangely, then continued with her lecture. "We're going to make sorbet out of mango, pineapple, and other tropical fruits," she said. "Then I'm going to show you a way of serving the sorbet very beautifully, similar to what we did with the white chocolate mousse."

Following Alicia's sorbet-making instructions, Nancy poured bits of fresh pineapple, corn syrup, and lemon juice into a blender and pressed the button. Watching the pale yellow mixture whirring around, she thought about the conversation she'd had on the phone with Officer Reed just before class. The police hadn't found fingerprints on the knife. But he'd told Nancy that he was keeping his eye on Alicia.

"The scarf business makes me suspicious," he'd said. "I'm going to bring her in for more questioning."

Was Officer Reed right? Nancy wondered. Should she, too, be putting the chef from New Orleans at the top of her suspect list?

During their conversation, Nancy had almost told Officer Reed about what happened to her the night before, but then decided against it. He was bound to give her a fatherly—and unwelcome—lecture about leaving police work to the police.

Alicia's voice broke into Nancy's thoughts just then. "I think you've blended your pineapple mixture long enough," she was saying.

Nancy started. Alicia was standing right beside her, watching her curiously.

"Thanks," Nancy said, turning off her blender. Alicia nodded and moved across the aisle to Paul. "Here, let me help you with that," she called out to him.

After everybody's sorbet mixtures were put into the freezer to solidify, Alicia went on to the next lesson.

"To serve the sorbet, we're going to make cookie tulips," Alicia announced. "The first step is to bake some big, round, thin cookies. Then, while the cookies are still warm and soft, we'll drape them over tin cans and pinch their sides down until they look like tulips."

"Isn't this fun?" Teddy Angell remarked to Nancy across the counter.

Gloria, who was working next to Teddy, said, "Frankly, I wish she'd give us more challenging assignments. I've done this tulip thing before."

Alicia walked over to the main oven and turned it on to 375 degrees. "While this is preheating, we'll make the cookie batter," she told the class.

A few minutes later Alicia was showing the students how to separate egg whites from their yolks. Suddenly she stopped and began sniffing suspiciously.

"What's that funny smell?" she murmured, then glanced at the oven. "Is something burning? But there's nothing in there."

Nancy sniffed the air, too, but she didn't smell anything strange. She was a good twenty feet away from the oven, though.

Alicia put down her egg and hurried over to the oven. She bent over to look through the glass in the oven door, then, frowning, she opened it.

Kaboom! An enormous cloud of smoke and debris blasted into the air. Alicia went flying backward against her worktable, her arms flailing helplessly.

7

The Circle Widens

Someone began screaming, and several of the students began stampeding toward the door. Unfazed by the chaos, Nancy rushed to Alicia's side. The chef was lying on the floor, looking dazed. Just a few feet away, black smoke continued to pour from the oven.

Nancy knelt down and glanced at Alicia anxiously. "Are you all right?"

Alicia sat up slightly and studied her arms, which were covered with soot and tiny red scratches. "I'm dirty and a little beat up, but otherwise I seem to be fine."

Nancy nodded. "In that case, stay put. I've got to take care of that oven."

Leaping to her feet, Nancy grabbed a fire extinguisher off a nearby wall and stood in front of the smoking oven. Reaching for a thick, padded pot holder, she opened the oven door and began spraying, shielding her eyes with one arm as she did so. Within seconds she had the fire under control.

"Are you okay, Nan?" she heard George call out from somewhere behind her. "Is there anything Bess and I can do?"

"Open all the windows!" Nancy shouted over her shoulder, keeping the spray of the fire extinguisher on the oven. "We need some fresh air in here, and fast!"

A few minutes later the smoke had subsided. Nancy put the fire extinguisher down. Her eyes stung, and her clothes were covered with soot.

George and Bess were helping Alicia to her feet.

"How are you doing, Alicia?" Nancy called out. "Should we call a doctor?"

"Oh, no," Alicia protested. "Really. I'm okay." Using a corner of her apron, she brushed the soot off her cheek. "How about that oven, though?" she asked Nancy worriedly. "Should we call the fire department?"

"I don't think it's necessary," Nancy said. "I managed to put everything out."

"We should at least tell Sophie," Bess added. "She'll need to know that she's got some very defective kitchen equipment."

"I don't think the explosion was caused by any defect," Nancy said slowly. She reached inside the oven with the pot holder and extracted a large, charred metal fragment. "My guess is that someone put an aerosol can in here sometime before class started. When you turned the oven on, Alicia, pressure built up inside the can until it blew up."

Alicia's brown eyes grew wide. "An aerosol can? Someone put it there on purpose?"

Nancy nodded.

Alicia was silent for a minute. "So whoever is after Regis has decided to come after me now," she said finally. "It's a nightmare."

Nancy glanced around the smoky room. The cold air blowing through the windows was gradually clearing the air. She, George, Bess, and Alicia were the only people there. Everyone else had left, apparently frightened by the explosion.

Nancy turned to her companions. "Alicia, we'd better get you up to your room. Then the rest of us are going to go break the bad news to Sophie."

By lunchtime Sophie was at the end of her rope. The police had announced to her that they were mounting a full investigation of the week's suspicious events. Sophie had then received a call from a reporter at the *Putney Grove Herald* who'd heard that a maniac was terrorizing the institute. Then two of the cooking club people had marched into her office, announced that they were leaving immediately, and demanded refunds.

70

"This is terrible," Sophie said to Nancy, Bess, and George. The four of them were sitting in her office discussing the case. Behind her desk, Sophie looked pale and tense.

"My school is going to be ruined," she went on. "Not to mention the fact that a crazy person is after Regis and Alicia. And you, too, Nancy!" she added unhappily. After the police left, Nancy had filled Sophie in on last night's attack by the cellar door.

Nancy frowned. "I don't know. The aerosol can in Alicia's oven could mean a lot of different things."

"Like what?" George asked.

Nancy looked at George and Bess, who sat on either side of her on Sophie's pink leather couch. Then she turned her gaze back to Sophie. "Regis could have done it to get back at Alicia," she suggested. "In his mind she's responsible for the poisoned salad and the knife attack."

"Do you really think he'd go that far?" Sophie asked her anxiously.

"Maybe," Nancy replied. "Another possibility is that our culprit—call him or her X—has been after Regis all along, and put the can in Alicia's oven just to throw us off track."

"The reverse could be true, too," George piped up. "Maybe X was after Alicia all along, and the two attacks against Regis were the smoke screens."

Nancy nodded. "That's right. And there could be

71

another, more dangerous possibility." She took a deep breath. "Maybe X is after anyone, or everyone, here. Maybe the attacks against Regis and Alicia and me are just the tip of the iceberg."

"If that's the case, I'm sending everybody home," Sophie moaned. "And then I'm going to crawl under the covers and never come out."

"I don't think that'll be necessary," Nancy said. "We just have to think hard and work fast, so we can catch X before he or she does any more harm."

"Do you have any idea who X is, if it's not Alicia?" Sophie asked her.

Nancy told her her suspicions about Lila and Paul. "Lila was acting very strangely when I ran into her in the north wing corridor. And she was obviously lying about what she was doing there," she concluded.

Nancy paused, then continued. "As for Paul, it's a bunch of little things. One, he can't seem to cook, even though he's a contest winner. Two, Regis has been giving him a lot of grief, which would give Paul a motive for the poisoned salad and the knife attack. And three, his application form is weird— there's not much on it.

"But at this point, I don't have any proof against either one of them," Nancy continued. "Plus, Paul has an airtight alibi for last night at eleven. And I haven't been able to come up with a motive for Lila."

The phone rang just then. Sophie picked it up. "Hello, Wolfe Culinary Institute," she said crisply. "Excuse me, what? What paper are you calling from? No, I will *not* give you a statement." She slammed the phone down.

"This institute's image is going down the drain," she announced grimly to the girls.

"How did the papers find out about what's going on here, anyway?" Nancy asked curiously.

Sophie shrugged. "Who knows? The grapevine, I suppose. Bad news always seems to travel quickly, don't you think?"

Nancy didn't reply.

"So what's the plan?" George asked once the three girls were back in their room. They were sitting cross-legged on the Oriental rug. The February sun filled the room with a hazy glow.

Nancy was making a list of all the suspects and their possible motives. "I have this hunch," she said slowly. "What if whoever is behind these attacks isn't out to kill or hurt anyone?"

Bess's blue eyes grew wide. "Have you gone off the deep end, Nan?" she exclaimed. "This person poisons Regis's salad, throws a huge knife at him, whacks you on the head, and makes Alicia's oven explode—and you don't think he or she is dangerous?"

"I see your point," Nancy said, her lips curling

up in a hint of a smile. "But the fact remains that Regis, Alicia, and I are all fine."

"So what are you saying, Nancy?" George asked.

"Maybe our culprit—let's keep calling him or her X—isn't necessarily trying to hurt Regis or Alicia or me," Nancy mused. "Maybe X just wants to scare one of us in a big way."

"Or maybe X is trying to scare us all," George added.

"But why?" Bess asked, puzzled.

Nancy sighed. "I don't know. That's what we've got to find out."

"So what do we do next?" George asked Nancy.

"I'm stumped for now," Nancy confessed. "George, why don't you go keep an eye on Lila? And, Bess, why don't you see how Alicia is doing?" She stood up and tugged at her baggy green sweater. "I'm going to question Regis again. Maybe now he'll see that someone besides Alicia might be after him. And then I want to talk to Paul White."

Nancy found Regis in room 11 preparing for the afternoon's cake-decorating class. He was pouring heavy cream into a chilled metal bowl.

"Of course Alicia Jones put that can in her own oven," Regis replied in answer to Nancy's question about the morning's incident. "Any fool could see that."

"But why would she have opened the oven door, knowing the can would blow up?" Nancy asked

74

him. "Wouldn't she have tried to get as far away from it as she could?"

Regis began whipping the cream with a high-speed beater. "That shows how devious she is," he said loudly.

"Don't you think it's possible that someone else is involved, though?" Nancy asked him in an equally loud voice. It was hard trying to carry on a conversation above the din of the beater. "Even if that's a slim possibility, isn't it worth considering? Your safety may depend on it."

The two corgis, who'd been asleep nearby, had awakened. Agitated by the noise, they ran over to Nancy and began nipping lightly at her heels.

"Hey!" Nancy cried out. "Stop that! What are you guys doing?"

Regis switched off the beater. "Peaches! Truffles! Stop that immediately!" The dogs looked up at him dolefully, then retreated. "The corgi is a sheep-herding dog," he explained unapologetically to Nancy. "When he senses trouble, his instinct is to nip at the heels of the sheep, to get them under control. In this case, you are the sheep."

Regis dipped a finger into the bowl of cream and tasted it. "Now, what were we talking about? Oh, yes, Alicia's clever criminal mind—"

"You've known Alicia for a while, right?" Nancy broke in.

"We've run into each other at various culinary conferences. And I've been to her so-called restaurant in New Orleans." Regis sniffed. "She is definitely a menace. If I were Sophie, I would have her escorted off the premises."

It was obvious to Nancy that she wasn't going to get anywhere with Regis.

"Excuse me," she murmured with a smile. "I just remembered that I have to take care of something." She turned to go, hoping the corgis wouldn't go after her heels again.

"Don't forget, class at four!" she heard Regis call after her.

Heading for the lobby, Nancy got the notion to ask Sophie a few more questions. Possibly X had some sort of gripe against the institute or against Sophie. If that were the case, Nancy needed some more information about them both.

When Nancy reached Sophie's office, she found the door closed. She raised her hand to knock, then stopped. There was a voice coming from inside. It was a male voice—Baird Goldensen's.

"Do you really think so?" he was saying.

Hearing no reply, Nancy realized that Baird was talking on the phone. But what was he doing in Sophie's office? she wondered. Didn't he have his own phone?

Nancy glanced around quickly to see if anyone was coming down the hall. Then she pressed her ear firmly to the door.

"It's fine," she heard Baird say. "She's not here right now."

Nancy frowned. What was going on? What was he discussing that he didn't want Sophie to overhear?

Her curiosity was aroused even more by Baird's next words.

"It won't be long now," he said with an ominous laugh. "The way things are going, Sophie Wolfe is sure to throw in the towel soon."

8

A Bloody Message

Nancy stepped back from the door, her mind racing. Could Baird be the one behind all the incidents? Was he trying to sabotage the institute for some reason?

She remembered meeting Baird in the living room, just before dinner on Monday night. When George had asked him if he worked for Sophie, he'd corrected her, saying that he worked *with* Sophie. Was he unhappy with his second-in-command status at the institute? Was he trying to run Sophie out of the place so he'd be able to fill her shoes?

Anxious to hear more, Nancy pressed her ear against the door again. Baird was talking about something else: an upcoming snowstorm.

Nancy knocked. After a long pause, Baird said, "Come in."

Nancy entered the room and saw Baird sitting on the edge of Sophie's desk, looking flushed. He had hung up the phone.

"Ms. Drew," he said coolly. "What can I do for you? Sophie's not here right now."

"I can see that," Nancy replied. "I'm sorry— maybe I'm disturbing you. I thought I heard you on the phone."

Nancy thought she noted a glimmer in his pale blue eyes. Was it fear? Hurriedly, he replied, "Yes, but I'm finished now. I was just taking a call for Sophie." His eyes shifted, glancing at a clock on the wall. "If you'll excuse me, it's time for my afternoon walk. Sophie should be back shortly."

With that, he stood up and strolled past Nancy and out the door.

Nancy stood there for a second, thinking. Then she had an idea and raced upstairs. Five minutes later she was tramping over the snow-covered front lawn, dressed in her parka and ski mittens, following Baird.

"Mr. Goldensen!" she cried out. Baird, who was wearing a long gray overcoat and black leather gloves, whirled around. "I thought I'd tag along with you," she explained. "I've been wanting to see more of these wonderful grounds."

"Indeed," Baird said curtly. Nancy could tell

that he was looking for a polite way to get rid of her. "It's awfully cold out here today," he said finally.

Nancy smiled. "Actually, I like the cold."

"Yes, well . . ." Baird dug his hands into the pockets of his coat and began walking briskly.

They soon reached the woods at the edge of the lawn. Several trails led off into the trees. Baird chose the westernmost one.

"It goes down to the river," he mumbled to Nancy in explanation. "I enjoy the river in winter, but some people are frightened by it. One can freeze to death in its icy waters in just minutes, you know."

Nancy stared at him. Why was he telling her this? She decided to change the subject. "So—speaking of being frightened, isn't it scary what's been going on here this week?"

"Sheer carelessness," Baird said, huffing. "If Sophie were more careful about the students she accepts—"

"So you think it's one of the students?" Nancy cut in. "But who?"

"I have no idea," Baird said. "I'm merely stating that Sophie should screen students better. These special-event weeks attract all sorts of riffraff, in my opinion." He gazed meaningfully at Nancy over the top of his tortoiseshell glasses.

He then turned his attention to the scenery around them. "It's so quiet here," he said, inhaling deeply. "And so desolate. If you look back, you'll see that the house is completely out of our view."

Nancy could tell she wasn't going to learn much from him. "I think I'll head back now," she said, stopping in her tracks. "I have to talk to Sophie before Regis's class. Thanks for the tour." She turned to go.

"I hope you can find your way back by yourself," Baird called after her.

Walking back to the building, Nancy was deep in thought. She had to get more information about Baird from Sophie. There was no mistake about the phone conversation she'd overheard. Baird was guilty of something—the question was, what?

Sophie was back in her office when Nancy reached it. "Why, hello," she said to Nancy, glancing up from a pile of papers. "You look like you've been outside. Did you have fun?"

"Not exactly," Nancy said, unzipping her parka and sitting down on the pink leather couch.

She told Sophie about Baird's peculiar phone conversation. To her surprise, Sophie didn't seem to be fazed by it.

"I'm sure you just heard it out of context," Sophie said, shrugging. "He was probably discussing my troubles with someone in a sympathetic way. You know, like, 'poor Sophie Wolfe is going to be forced to throw in the towel soon if these terrible things don't stop.'"

Nancy frowned. "He didn't sound very sympathetic to me," she said. "And besides, why was he using your phone?"

"We often answer each other's calls," Sophie replied. "He was probably in here and happened to pick it up.

"Maybe he didn't sound very sympathetic," Sophie added. "Baird isn't a particularly warm person. In fact, he's quite shy. But he's extremely loyal. He would never go behind my back."

Nancy considered telling Sophie about Baird's disapproving comment regarding the special-event weeks, but she decided against it. Sophie seemed certain of Baird's loyalty, and Nancy had no real proof to convince her otherwise.

"Okay," Nancy conceded. "Anyway, the reason I came by earlier was to ask you a question. Do you have any enemies that you know of?"

"I should hope not," Sophie replied, looking startled. "Why do you ask?"

"I have a theory that X—our mystery person—isn't after Alicia or Regis specifically but has some grand scheme in mind. The grand scheme could be to bring you down," Nancy said slowly.

"What an awful thought," Sophie murmured. "But as far as I know, I've never made any enemies —or given anyone a reason to hold a grudge against me."

Nancy nodded. "What about the institute? Maybe someone wants the building itself? Have you had any offers to buy it over the last few years?"

Sophie shook her head. "Do you think someone might be trying to scare me into selling?"

"It was just an idea," Nancy said. "What about your competition? There are a lot of other cooking schools, right? You've mentioned the Leblanc and the Metzger—didn't you say you're surpassing them in enrollment?"

Sophie laughed disbelievingly. "You make it sound like I'm part of some high-powered, cut-throat industry," she said. "Culinary institutes don't operate that way. I can't imagine my competitors sending henchmen to destroy my business simply because my enrollment is up."

Just then the phone rang. "I have to take this," Sophie said apologetically. "I'm expecting an important call."

Nancy stood up. "I should be going, anyway. Regis's class is at four o'clock."

Picking up her ski mittens, she said goodbye and headed for the door.

At that moment she glimpsed a flash of yellow just outside the doorway.

Curious, Nancy rushed out into the hall. A guy with dark wavy hair was walking away at a brisk pace. It was Paul White, dressed in a bright yellow sweater and jeans.

Nancy's eyes widened. Had he been eavesdropping on her conversation with Sophie?

"Paul!" she called out.

He stopped abruptly and turned around. "Oh, hello," he said with a thin smile. "Nancy, right?"

"Right," she said, catching up to him. "Did you want to talk to Sophie? I saw you standing outside her door."

Paul's handsome face clouded over for a second. Nancy watched him intently, wondering what he would say next.

"Um, I was just looking for someone to play pool with," he replied after a moment. "I heard that Baird Goldensen was good, and I thought he might be around."

"I'll play with you," she volunteered, wanting the opportunity to spend some time with Paul. "We've got half an hour until Regis's class—enough for a quick game."

Paul looked surprised. "Oh, that's all right," he mumbled.

"It'll be fun," Nancy insisted, taking his arm and steering him into the rec room.

In the wood-paneled rec room, Nancy studied Paul as he lifted several pool cues from the wall rack. What was this guy's story? she wondered. She was sure that he'd been listening in while she and Sophie discussed the case. Why? Was it just curiosity—or something more?

Paul's voice interrupted her thoughts. "Ready to play?" he asked.

After the first few shots, Paul said, "You're better

than I thought you'd be. Funny, you don't look like the pool-playing type."

"I guess that's a compliment," Nancy murmured, lining up a particularly difficult shot. She pulled her cue stick back, paused, then thrust it forward smoothly, making contact. The white cue ball zoomed across the table and hit the three ball at a sharp angle, sending it spinning into one of the corner pockets.

She stood up and chalked the tip of her cue. "So why don't I look like the pool-playing type?" she asked Paul.

"I don't know," Paul said, shrugging. "You're a girl, for one thing."

Nancy grinned. "Didn't your father and mother raise you to believe that women can do anything men can?"

Paul's face darkened. "My mother died when I was young," he muttered.

"I'm sorry," Nancy said, taken aback. "I know what that's like. I lost my mother when I was three." She added, "I was raised by my dad. I suppose you were, too?"

The question seemed to strike yet another nerve. Paul put his cue down on the table and mumbled, "It's getting late." He turned and marched out the door.

"Poor Paul," Bess murmured, trying to run a comb through her hair. There were clumps of whipped cream and frosting stuck in it; her beater had gone out of control during Regis's cake-decorating class. "He doesn't look like a very happy person."

"He may come from a tough family situation," Nancy conceded, slipping a silver necklace over her head. "But that doesn't explain why he was eavesdropping on me and Sophie. Or why there's almost no information about him on his application form. Or why he can't seem to cook even though he won a recipe contest."

George opened the girls' closet door and studied its contents. "But you have to admit, Nan, none of those things mean he's a crazy, knife-wielding maniac," she called over her shoulder. "For that matter, neither do the things you've told us about Baird."

"I know it," Nancy said with a sigh. "I need some proof against one of them or against Lila or Alicia. And I can't seem to get my hands on any clues."

George turned around. "I think you need a little break from mystery solving," she said. "And I know just the thing. It's supposed to snow tonight."

"So?" Bess said.

"So we can all go cross-country skiing in the morning," George said excitedly. "They've got some great trails here. And speaking for myself, I'm looking forward to working off some of the rich food we've been eating."

"That does sound like fun," Nancy agreed. She

peered at her watch. "Hey, we'd better finish getting changed. Dinner's about to start."

"You guys go on," Bess muttered, throwing her comb down on the dressing table. "I can't go down looking like this. I'll have to wash my hair."

"You'd better make it fast, or there won't be any food left," George teased.

Downstairs Nancy and George were following a crowd of people into the dining hall. The delicious aroma of roast chicken, garlic, and herbs filled the air.

"Whoa, that smells great," said Teddy Angell, who was right behind Nancy and George.

Just then the first people entering the dining hall jerked to a sudden halt. Nancy heard Lila Barnstable gasp, "Oh, no!"

Nancy pushed her way to the front of the crowd to see what was the matter.

On the far wall, facing them, big red letters oozed and dripped like blood. The ominous message read: Who Will Be Next?

A shocked silence fell over the crowd.

Then the silence was interrupted by a piercing scream from somewhere upstairs. Nancy threw George a look of alarm.

"That sounded like Bess!" Nancy cried out.

9

Terror in the Snow

Nancy turned around and raced upstairs. George was at her heels.

They found Bess huddled on the bathroom floor, looking frightened. A strange burning smell hung in the air.

Nancy crouched down beside Bess. "Are you all right?" she asked her worriedly.

"I-I'm okay," Bess said shakily.

"What happened?" George murmured, putting a hand on her cousin's shoulder.

"That thing gave me a shock." Bess pointed to her hair dryer, which had fallen on the floor. An extension cord connected it to a wall outlet above the sink.

Nancy got up and peered at the extension cord. It

looked flimsy and worn, and on part of it the plastic coating had melted off, exposing the wire underneath.

"Bess, you should never use a hair dryer with an extension cord, especially a beat-up cord like this," Nancy scolded her. "See how the plastic coating's melting off?"

"Don't you think I know that?" Bess protested. "That's not my extension cord—I've never seen it before in my life."

"Are you saying that somebody *put* it there?" George asked, perching on the edge of the bathtub.

Bess stood up slowly and sank down next to George. "What other explanation could there be? The last time I used my hair dryer was this morning. It was plugged directly into the wall then." She sighed impatiently. "It didn't occur to me to inspect it before I used it again."

Nancy reached over and unplugged the extension cord swiftly. "At what point did you get shocked?" she asked Bess.

"I'm not sure," said Bess, trying to recall. "I had the hair dryer on for a few minutes when I started smelling a funny plastic smell. I didn't think anything of it at the time. I must have accidentally touched the exposed wire." Bess paused, shuddering. "It was awful." Then she broke into a sheepish smile. "I bet everybody heard me scream, huh?"

Nancy looked thoughtful. "Listen, this is probably another attempt by X to scare me off the case. If

X doesn't think it worked, he or she might get really desperate."

"Then X will pull out all the stops and do even scarier, more horrible things to you," George said.

"X can't get me if I'm careful," Nancy stated firmly. "And if X goes to greater lengths to chase me away, I'll have a better chance at catching him or her in the act. Don't you see?"

"So what are you proposing?" George asked.

Nancy turned to Bess. "Pretend this didn't happen. When we get downstairs, say . . . say you saw a mouse, or you thought you did. Okay?"

Fluffing her damp blond hair with her fingers, Bess rolled her eyes and smirked. "The helpless-girl-screaming-at-the-mouse routine. Sure, why not? It works in the movies." Her spirits were already bouncing back after the scare.

"Now let's get downstairs and see about that blood on the wall," Nancy said, heading for the bathroom door.

"Blood on the wall?" Bess shrieked. "What is she talking about, George?"

When Nancy got downstairs, Sophie told her that the "blood" was actually icing colored with red food dye. Nancy remembered that the class had made red icing that afternoon for a Valentine's Day cake.

As Nancy and Sophie studied the ominous message, Sophie whispered, "I've managed to calm everybody down, I think. But I don't know how much more they can take."

Nancy glanced around the dining hall. People were sitting at the tables picking at the food on their plates, making stilted, anxious conversation.

Bess and George had joined Baird and Alicia. "You don't understand," Bess was saying to Baird. "I only *thought* I saw a mouse. No, please don't call the exterminator. It's just me—I must need glasses." She tittered nervously.

Nancy turned to Sophie. "Did you question the people in the kitchen?" she asked in a low voice. "Did any of them see anything?"

"From six-fifty to seven o'clock, they were all in the kitchen," Sophie replied. "Audrey, one of the assistants, came out at seven on the dot, she says, to check on the table settings. She spotted the writing on the wall and went to fetch Louis Drake. Just then all the diners came into the room and saw it themselves."

"This was obviously done with a pastry tube, like the kind we used in cake-decorating class today," Nancy said, nodding at the red scrawl. "It wouldn't have taken more than a minute. Still, it was a big risk for our culprit to take. He or she could have been discovered pretty easily."

"All I know is, we have to catch this maniac soon," Sophie said heavily. "The rest of the

91

cooking-club people have told me they're leaving tomorrow. Between word of mouth and the newspapers, I'll be ruined for sure!"

Hours later after everyone had gone to bed, Nancy lay in the darkness thinking. The message on the wall seemed to suggest that her latest theory was right. X wasn't after Regis or Alicia but probably Sophie or the institute.

Mentally, Nancy ran down her list of suspects. First, there was Alicia. In light of the oven explosion, she didn't seem like such a strong candidate anymore. But Nancy knew it was too early to drop her from the list.

Lila, Baird, and Paul still seemed to be the most likely suspects. The trouble was that she had no proof against any of them. As far as motives went, she had slim ones for Paul and Baird, and none for Lila. And opportunity? Paul definitely could not have hit her on the head last night—he'd been playing cards with Taylor and Jamie.

When it came right down to it, Nancy thought, she had a lot of odds and ends that didn't add up to anything. Baird's phone conversation . . . Lila's excursion in the old hallway . . . Paul's application form . . . all three of them acting nervous and secretive . . .

It was past midnight before Nancy was able to drift off to sleep.

* * *

"The weather station said we got six inches of snow!" George whooped, turning off the clock radio on her nightstand. "This is fantastic!"

Nancy sat up in bed and stretched lazily. "What's fantastic?" she murmured, yawning.

George jumped out of bed and ran to the window. "Come and look at this, Nan."

After another stretch, Nancy joined George. Outside, everything was covered by a dazzling blanket of snow: the lawn, the trees, and the riverbanks beyond. The morning sun made the white landscape shimmer.

"It's beautiful," Nancy agreed. "Nothing but white as far as the eye can see." She paused and leaned forward. "Except that little dot over there. Is that a person?" She pointed to a spot near the edge of the woods.

George squinted. "That looks like Gloria Chen. And she's skiing! I can't believe someone beat me to the trails."

"What's going on?" A sleepy voice came from under a pile of blankets on Bess's bed. "What's everybody doing up in the middle of the night?"

"Good morning, Sleeping Beauty," George crooned. "Rise and shine. Time to go cross-country skiing."

Bess sat up and scowled at George. "You woke me up so that I could climb some icy, hilly trails with a couple of sticks and poles?" she exclaimed. "You've got to be kidding. There is no way you're going to get me out there!''

But at breakfast Bess had a change of heart. Gloria was organizing a group ski outing for after class, and Paul was one of the first to sign up.

"So you're a skier?" Bess said to Paul, setting her breakfast plate down at his table. "Maybe you could give me some pointers, then. I'm an amateur.''

"We should all go out,'' Gloria said. She was sitting with George, Nancy, and Alicia. "There's a bunch of equipment in the rec room closet. And if anyone can't find the right-size boots or skis or poles, I'm sure we could rent some in town.''

Nancy bit down on a zucchini muffin and frowned. As much as she wanted to go skiing, she felt she ought to be working on the case instead.

"I'm not sure I'll be able to go—'' she began.

"Oh, but you must!'' Gloria interrupted, leaning forward. "The snow is incredible. We can all go on the trail I skied this morning—you know, the hilly one that's closest to the road.''

"I suppose I could go for a short run,'' Nancy relented.

"I insist on it,'' Gloria said.

Nancy looked at her curiously and took a thoughtful sip of tea.

The wind whipped Nancy's reddish blond hair as she coasted down a gentle hill. She went into a slight tuck to gain some speed.

94

"This is great!" she called to Paul, who was skiing right behind her.

Besides Nancy and Paul, the group consisted of George, Bess, Alicia, Lila, and Gloria. George had lagged behind to help Alicia, who was struggling to stay on her feet. Gloria was also at the rear of the line, coaching Lila and Bess.

"You two go up front," Gloria had told Paul and Nancy. "I'll stay behind. I already had one good run today."

The group followed Gloria's early morning tracks, which cut deep into the six inches of fresh snow. The trail twisted this way and that through the beautiful, sun-dappled woods. White powder sprinkled from the tree branches as the skiers whooshed past.

Paul and Nancy reached the base of another hill. Nancy pointed her skis into a V shape and began to climb, using her poles to help pull herself up.

Near the top she heard Paul mutter, "This is exhausting."

Nancy soon reached the top and started her descent. Her shoulders ached slightly from the climb up, and she was glad to be going downhill.

She went into another tuck. Just as she gained momentum, Nancy suddenly realized that the trail was about to curve sharply to the right. Thinking quickly, she straightened out of the tuck and formed a wedge shape with her skis in an effort to slow down.

But she couldn't slow down fast enough.

The next few seconds were like a bad dream. As she sped into the curve, Nancy's skis hit something hard and unyielding on the ground. The next thing she knew, she was flying through the air, totally out of control!

10

Truffles Is Missing

"I think she's coming to."

Nancy blinked. There were faces swimming above her. She squinted, trying to see better. A blonde and a brunette were hovering over her.

"Bess?" Nancy whispered. "George?"

"She's awake, Dr. Reynolds." It was Bess's voice, loud and exuberant. "Nan, can you hear me? You're going to be fine."

Nancy's eyes were finally focusing properly. She realized that she was in the girls' room, lying in bed under a quilt. Bess and George sat beside her. Standing behind them were Sophie and a young woman with a stethoscope around her neck.

The young woman leaned forward. "I'm Dr.

Reynolds, Nancy," she said. "You've had a nasty spill, but you're going to be okay. I just want to check you out a little more and ask you a few questions."

While Dr. Reynolds was examining her, Bess and George filled her in on what had happened. "You and Paul had gone over the hill already—the rest of us were still climbing up," Bess recounted. "Then suddenly we heard Paul call out for help. Gloria and George went ahead, leaving the rest of us weaklings at the bottom."

"You were lying in the snow, unconscious," George continued. "Paul got your skis off—"

"—and he carried you all the way back to the house in his arms," Bess added.

Dr. Reynolds put her instruments back in her black leather bag. "You seem to be fine, Nancy," she said cheerfully, then added in a more serious tone of voice, "But you're going to have to take it easy for a little while. I'm prescribing bed rest for you for the remainder of today and tonight. And when I say bed rest, I mean bed rest. I want you to take all your meals in here."

"I'll make the arrangements right away," Sophie said, heading for the door.

"We'll make sure she stays in bed, Dr. Reynolds," George said firmly.

After the doctor left, Nancy said, "George, Bess, I want you to go back to that spot on the trail right away."

"You mean the place where you went flying through the air?" Bess asked.

Nancy tried to sit up. George adjusted the pillows behind her head. "That's right," Nancy said. "I want you to inspect that trail carefully. Check for anything strange."

"Like an obstruction?" George asked. "Are you saying that you think your accident wasn't an accident?"

"My skis hit something before I went out of control," Nancy explained. "I want to know what it was—and if it was put there intentionally."

George and Bess came back an hour later. Nancy was sitting up in bed looking at her notes on the case. She saw the grim looks on her friends' faces. "You guys found something, didn't you?"

They sat down on the edge of her bed. "Bricks," George announced gravely.

"What?" Nancy asked in surprise.

"We found some bricks in a neat little row across the trail right where you fell," Bess explained. "No wonder you didn't see them there—they were hidden under the snow."

"We didn't find any clues as to who put them there, though," George added. "No weird footprints or anything like that."

Nancy was silent. "X strikes again," she said finally. "Of course, those bricks couldn't have been meant for me specifically. Any one of us could have gotten to that spot first."

"But Gloria sent you and Paul ahead of the rest of us," Bess reminded her.

Nancy frowned. "True. And it was Gloria who convinced me to go skiing in the first place. I was going to spend the morning working on the case, but she was so persistent . . ."

"And Gloria skied that trail earlier this morning," George added. "She could have planted the bricks while she was out there." She shook her head. "But why would she do such a thing?"

Nancy shrugged. "I don't know. I've got enough suspects to worry about without having to add Gloria to my list." She paused. "You have to admit that it's a weird coincidence."

"So what else is new?" Bess said, sighing. "This case is *full* of weird coincidences."

Nancy was back on her feet the next morning, although her body ached all over from the fall. After breakfast she decided to drive into the village of Putney Grove to get some ointment for her sore muscles.

Downtown Putney Grove consisted of a main street lined with stores and restaurants, all built in the Victorian style. After parking her Mustang and going to the pharmacy, Nancy strolled down the sidewalk, stopping occasionally to admire the colorful window displays.

One display in particular caught her attention. The Putney Grove Bookstore was advertising a half-price sale. In the window were samples of some of the bargain titles. Right up front was a pile of cookbooks by Gloria Chen.

Gloria said that her books were best-sellers, Nancy thought. Why would this store be trying to get rid of them at half price?

Curious, she decided to go inside and find out. The clerk smiled when Nancy brought up Gloria's name.

"Her books haven't sold well in about five or six years," he explained. "That's why they're in our sale. There are too many good cookbooks out there, and Gloria Chen's stuff can't compete."

As Nancy drove back to the institute, she reflected on Gloria's bragging about her success as an author. Obviously, she'd been stretching the truth. What was her real story, anyway?

Gripping the steering wheel tightly to maneuver an icy turn, Nancy's thoughts shifted to the skiing outing yesterday. Gloria had organized it so eagerly. Had she been involved in Nancy's "accident" somehow? Could she be X?

But Nancy had no proof, and she couldn't come up with a motive for Gloria. Once again, it was just odds and ends that didn't add up to anything.

During Alicia's pastry-making class later that morning, Nancy casually mentioned to Gloria that she'd seen her books in the half-price sale.

Gloria's amber eyes narrowed. "The manager obviously has no sense or taste," she said curtly.

"But weren't you saying the other day that your books are all best-sellers?" Nancy asked.

"How are you feeling, by the way?" Gloria said brightly, ignoring Nancy's question. "We were all so worried about you yesterday."

Just then Alicia began calling out some instructions to the class. Gloria turned away without waiting for a reply from Nancy.

"First word!" Teddy Angell shouted out. "Sounds like *hit!*"

Bess was acting out a charade for her team members, Teddy and Nancy. Shaking her head frantically, she began whacking the side of her right hand against her left arm. The other team, which consisted of George, Taylor, and Jamie, sprawled back on the living room couch, watching in amusement.

"Sounds like *chop!*" Nancy shouted out. Bess nodded vigorously. Nancy continued. "Hop, stop, shop—"

"My dog is missing!"

At the sound of Regis Brady's voice everyone turned to stare. The instructor stood in the living room doorway, his dark eyes full of fury.

"What do you mean, your dog is missing, Mr. Brady?" Bess said.

"I mean, my dog is missing," Regis repeated impatiently. "I shut Truffles and Peaches in my room before dinner, as I always do. But tonight, when I went upstairs, Truffles was gone! Only Peaches was there."

"Is there any way Truffles could have escaped?" Nancy spoke up. Regis shook his head. "How about your door? Was it locked?"

"No, but it was shut tight. A dog can't turn a doorknob," Regis said sarcastically. He sighed. "Perhaps I should call in the police, although they haven't exactly impressed me with their detective skills."

Nancy stood up. "Why don't we look for Truffles ourselves first?" she suggested in a calm voice. "That'll be faster. If we don't have any success, we'll call Officer Reed."

"Sounds like a good idea," Teddy chimed in.

"I suppose," Regis agreed reluctantly.

Nancy assigned everyone in the group to search a different part of the house and grounds. "George, you take the second floor, north wing. Bess, you take the south wing. I'll take the first floor, north wing, and Teddy, you take the south. Mr. Brady, you take the greenhouse. Taylor and Jamie, you can explore the grounds—if you don't mind the cold."

"No problem," Taylor said. "We'll just grab our coats and some flashlights and get going."

As everyone was heading out of the living room, Bess caught up to Nancy and whispered, "You don't think our crazy criminal X has kidnapped little Truffles, do you?"

"It's possible," Nancy whispered back.

On her way to the north wing, Nancy wondered who might have had the opportunity to steal Truffles. She tried to remember. Had anyone shown up late for dinner? Or left the dining hall during the meal? Nancy and the others had gone to the living room for charades after dinner, while Regis had lingered over dessert and coffee with Sophie. Perhaps X had used that opportunity to sneak up to Regis's room and lure Truffles away.

After searching through each of the classrooms in the north wing, Nancy came to the unrenovated part of the corridor. She heard a faint scratching sound coming from the wine cellar.

"Truffles?" she called out loudly.

In response, she got a sharp yip. Nancy rushed to the cellar door and yanked it open. The brown corgi came bounding out, panting happily.

Nancy knelt down and patted him. He jumped up on his short hind legs and licked her face.

"You're welcome, Truffles," Nancy said, laughing. "Now, if only you could tell me how you ended up down there, I could solve this case and call it a night."

Nancy carried Truffles to the greenhouse, where she found Regis stooping beside a jasmine bush. He held a can of Doggy De-Light dog food in his hand.

"Here, Truffles. Here—" Then Regis spotted Nancy and Truffles, and he broke into an ecstatic smile. "Ms. Drew, you found him! But where?"

Handing the dog back to his owner, Nancy explained the whole story. "I have a feeling the dognapper lured Truffles out of your room with food," she finished, glancing at the can Regis was holding. "Otherwise, there's no way anyone could have gotten him downstairs, down the north wing hall, and into the cellar without attracting attention. Truffles isn't exactly a quiet dog."

Regis raised his eyebrows at this but said nothing.

Regis and Nancy split up to tell the other searchers that Truffles had been found. They drifted back to the rec room, where Nancy recounted her story. Relieved and grateful, Regis thanked everyone for their efforts, then the party broke up and everyone went to bed.

Alone in their room, Nancy and the girls discussed Truffles's disappearance. "Who could have done it?" George mused, running a comb through her dark curls.

"Well, I know for a fact that it wasn't Paul," Bess said, smoothing cream onto her face.

"Why not?" Nancy asked her.

"He's got a cold," Bess replied. "I ran into him near the kitchen. He was getting a cup of herbal tea. He looked really sick to me—I can't imagine him sneaking around stealing—"

"Do you guys hear something?" Nancy asked suddenly.

Bess and George fell silent. "You mean that funny humming noise?" Bess said.

"I think I hear it, too," George added.

"It sounds like a radiator hissing or an electrical short," Nancy remarked, glancing around.

"Oh, no, not another defective extension cord," Bess moaned.

Nancy fixed her eyes on the closet door. "I think it's coming from in there," she said, walking toward it. "But that doesn't make sense . . ."

"Be careful, Nan," George said tensely. "What if it's a bomb or something?"

"Bombs don't make that kind of noise," Nancy told her, sliding the closet door open a crack. "It's probably just a—"

Then Nancy stopped—and gasped. Inside the closet swarmed a horde of angry honeybees!

11

Secrets from the Past

"Nan!" George shouted.

Nancy slammed the door shut quickly. "I don't believe it," she panted, turning to face her friends. "There are bees in there. A lot of them."

Bess gasped. "Bees!"

"But how did they—" George began.

"The beehive, remember?" Nancy cut in. "Sophie's got a beekeeping setup in the yard—she showed it to us the first day we were here. Someone must have moved a bunch of bees from there to here." She headed for the door. "Come on, let's get Sophie—she'll know what to do."

They found Sophie in her bedroom and explained the situation to her quickly.

"I don't believe it!" Sophie moaned. "Are you girls all right?"

Nancy nodded. "The question is, how did those bees get into our closet? And how do we get them out?"

Sophie grabbed her down coat, which was slung over the back of a chair. "Let's go out to the beehive—we'll find our solution there."

Once outside, Nancy scanned the ground with her flashlight. "No footprints," she noted. "Someone made an effort to brush them away."

Sophie leaned over and peered into the beehive, which was housed in a four-foot-high wooden case near the greenhouse. "It's been tampered with, all right," she remarked unhappily. "Most of the bees should be hibernating, but they're not. It's a mass of activity in there."

Bess drew the hood of her parka tighter around herself. "Will they come after us?"

"I doubt it," Sophie said. She reached behind the case, picked up something off the ground, and dusted the snow off it. It was a small box with a screen at one end of it and a lid at the other.

"This is a bee transporter—it's what we use to move bees from one place to another," Sophie explained. "I usually have two of them, but—" She glanced around. "One of them is missing. Our culprit must have used it to get the bees to your closet, then left the box in there with the lid open."

"So whoever did this had to be experienced with bees," Nancy remarked.

"That's right," Sophie replied. "This person is either a professional beekeeper or keeps bees for a hobby."

"Does anyone here know beekeeping besides you?" George spoke up.

Sophie shook her head. "As far as I know, I'm the only staff member who can handle these bees."

Back in the girls' room, Sophie coaxed the bees into her transporter box—the queen bee leading the way—within twenty minutes. Once the closet was cleared they found the second box inside, with the lid open.

"That should do it," Sophie said, shutting the closet door. "But I'll be back to spray for stragglers, just to be sure."

After Sophie left with both transporters, Nancy and her friends sat down wearily on the floor.

"I wish we could find X soon," Bess said, sighing. "Getting electrocuted by my hair dryer and being attacked by bees is really putting a damper on my week."

"Yeah, those bees really got you good, didn't they?" George teased. Bess threw her hairbrush at George and then started laughing.

George threw it back and turned to Nancy. "Bess is right, though. X has us running around in circles while he—"

"—or she," Nancy cut in.

"—or she poisons Regis's salad, throws a ten-inch knife at him, bops you on the head, blows up Alicia's oven, writes scary things on the dining room wall, causes you to wipe out on the cross-country skiing trail, and kidnaps that hyper little dog," George finished. "Plus the stuff Bess mentioned."

"X has been one busy criminal," Nancy agreed. "And we're running out of time. It's Friday night already, and Monday is the last day of class."

"Well, after what we've been through, there's nowhere to go but up," Bess pronounced firmly. "I have a feeling we'll get our big break tomorrow."

Saturday morning only brought more bad news. As the girls were getting dressed for breakfast, Sophie came to the door holding a newspaper in her hand. She looked distressed.

"The *Putney Grove Herald* has printed a story about what's been going on here," Sophie wailed. "What am I going to do? My school will be ruined."

Nancy glanced at the title of the article: Country's Top Cooking School Vandalized. Skimming the first few paragraphs, she noted that the reporter had described X's escapades with great accuracy.

"I don't understand how the writer got all these details," Nancy said, frowning. She looked up at

Bess and George. "Let's go down and grab a bite, then try and track down this reporter's source."

"But reporters don't have to reveal their sources," Bess pointed out.

"True, but if we're tricky, we might get it out of him anyway." Nancy glanced back at the paper. "It looks like X's work to me. If he or she is trying to sabotage this place, getting this story in the paper is a great way to do it."

As the four of them headed downstairs, they passed a phone booth in the hallway. Nancy noticed that Paul was inside talking to someone on the phone. He clutched a copy of the morning paper in his hand. He looks upset, Nancy thought. What could be the matter with him?

Sophie headed for her office, and Nancy and the girls went into the dining hall. After filling their plates with food, they joined Lila, who was sitting alone.

"Good morning," Lila said, glancing up quickly from her bowl of fresh fruit. "How are you feeling today, Nancy? Do you think you're fully recovered from your skiing accident?"

Nancy studied the older woman carefully. She seemed sincerely concerned. "I'm fine, thanks," she responded.

Just then Paul came barging into the room, his face dark with anger. He grabbed a poppyseed muffin from the buffet, then sat down at the next table. Slouching low in his seat, he began eating the muffin sullenly.

Lila leaned over. "Are you all right?" she asked Paul softly.

Paul stared at her. "It's nothing," he mumbled. "Just my father. He's got to be the most—"

Then a wary look crossed his green eyes, and he clammed up. "Like I said, it's nothing," he said, and turned back to his muffin.

It must have been his father he was talking to on the phone, Nancy thought.

Paul's reluctance to open up didn't stop Lila. She nodded, half at him and half at the girls. "Problems with your dad, huh?" she murmured. "I understand perfectly. I had a tough relationship with my father, too, when he was alive."

Nancy noticed that Lila's eyes were misting slightly. "No one could ever say that Lawrence Fairgate was an easy man to live with," Lila went on, her voice full of emotion. "But we don't choose our parents, do we?"

Nancy's hand, which was holding a buttered English muffin, stopped in midair. Lawrence Fairgate, Lila had said. The name rang a bell. But where had Nancy heard it before?

Then it came to Nancy. She'd run across the name Fairgate somewhere among the dusty files in the old office.

Paul stood up suddenly. "I've got to run," he muttered.

After he left, Nancy also rose to her feet. "I've got to run, too," she said to Lila.

"Nan, where are you—" Bess began.

"Just a little errand," Nancy responded hastily, walking away. "I'll see you guys later."

Nancy headed for the old office, her mind racing excitedly. The name Fairgate had appeared in an article about the institute, she recalled. Could Lila's family have a hidden connection with the school?

In the office, Nancy flipped on a light switch and headed for the boxes of old files. Reaching into a box, she picked up some of the folders she'd looked at with Bess on Wednesday.

Within minutes she found the article she wanted. She skipped down to the second paragraph. "The mansion was originally owned by the Fairgate family," it said. "Its first owner, Theodore Fairgate, passed it on to his son Lawrence sixty years ago, along with the family's vast steel fortune. But Lawrence, a notorious gambler who lost most of his inheritance at the race track, could not keep up with the property taxes and had to sell it after two decades. The building was taken over by the town, which turned it into a museum—"

Nancy put the article down slowly. The mansion was Lila's childhood home, she realized. Her father had been forced to give it up—probably when Lila was a teenager, she concluded, making a quick calculation in her head.

Nancy frowned. Lila had returned to Fairgate Mansion without telling anyone she was a Fairgate. But why all the secrecy?

Just then Nancy heard a noise. Someone was walking down the corridor toward the office. It could be Bess or George or Sophie, she thought, but she wasn't going to take any chances. She stood up silently, shut off the light, and hid behind a filing cabinet in the corner.

A second later the door opened slowly—and in slipped Gloria Chen.

12

Lila's Story

Peeking around the corner of the file cabinet, Nancy watched as Gloria closed the door behind her and then snapped on the light. What on earth was she up to?

Clutching a large beige shoulder bag, Gloria looked around the cramped, dusty room. Nancy instinctively flattened her body against the wall. She hoped Gloria hadn't spotted her.

A few seconds later Nancy could hear Gloria moving around. She decided to risk another peek. Much to her surprise, she saw Gloria bending over one of the boxes, thumbing through the old files. Gloria glanced over her shoulder toward the door constantly. She then tucked a few files into the shoulder bag, turned out the light, and tiptoed out the door.

As soon as the coast was clear, Nancy emerged quietly from her hiding place, brushing some dust off her jeans. She went over to the box Gloria had been going through. It contained files on a number of subjects—it was impossible to tell what Gloria had taken.

Now Nancy had *two* new leads to pursue: Lila's secret past and Gloria's mysterious file-smuggling!

Up in their room after Alicia's morning class, Nancy brought her friends up-to-date on the case.

"I want to go after Lila and Gloria this afternoon," Nancy finished.

"How can we help?" George asked eagerly.

"I need you two to follow another lead," Nancy replied. "Check up on the *Putney Grove Herald* story about the institute—head over to their office and find out who that reporter's source was. He may not tell you if you ask him directly, but maybe you can get a tidbit or two out of him."

After lunch Bess and George left for the *Herald* office, and Nancy went to find Lila. She discovered the older woman in the greenhouse, alone. Standing in the doorway unobserved, Nancy watched her wander from one plant to the next, touching them wistfully. When Lila paused in front of a spray of white orchids, Nancy came up behind her.

"Pretty, aren't they?" Nancy called out.

Lila whirled around, lifting a fluttering hand to her heart. "Oh, it's you," she said. "You frightened me."

Nancy smiled apologetically. "I'm sorry, I didn't mean to sneak up on you."

Lila turned back to the white orchids. "Do you know them, Nancy? Dendrobiums."

Nancy shook her head. "Did you learn about them in one of your courses?" she asked.

"No. My mother raised orchids when I was a little girl," Lila replied vaguely.

Nancy saw a chance to get Lila to reveal her identity. "This greenhouse really is great," she said, watching Lila carefully. "It's so nice Sophie decided to add it on when she bought the house."

"Oh, no," Lila responded instantly. "The greenhouse has been here since—"

She stopped and looked at Nancy, her eyes wide. Nancy stared back at her levelly.

After a moment Lila said, "You know who I am, don't you?"

Nancy nodded slowly.

Lila turned away from her and stared out at the garden. It had begun to snow outside. Tiny snowflakes fell on the greenhouse, melted instantly, and trickled in thin streams down the transparent walls.

"I loved this house," Lila said finally. "It broke my heart when my father lost it."

"That must have been terrible," Nancy sympathized.

"For a long time I didn't have the heart to come back," Lila continued. "But a few months ago I thought, why not? Signing up for this dessert week was a perfect opportunity. I could wander around the house as often as I wanted."

Nancy suddenly remembered the incident in the north wing corridor. "That afternoon, when I bumped into you by the cellar door—" she began.

Lila laughed softly. "When I was twelve, I scratched the initials of a boy I liked into the stone wall," she explained. "I was trying to find it when you happened upon me. I was so nervous . . . I didn't want you to know who I was."

"But why not?" Nancy asked, frowning.

Lila looked at Nancy squarely. "All through my childhood we were constantly hounded by creditors because of my father. Even our relatives stopped talking to us because he owed them so much money. I loved my father, Nancy, but I'm not proud to be his daughter. I had no intention of telling anyone here the story of my past."

"You don't have to worry, Lila," Nancy assured her. "Your secret is safe with me."

Nancy didn't see Bess and George until Regis's four o'clock class. They rushed in, five minutes into his lecture, still wearing their coats. Bess was carrying several shopping bags.

118

"There is a type of petit four known as the Fairy Cake— Oh, good afternoon, Ms. Marvin and Ms. Fayne," Regis called out. "Thank you for honoring us with your presence today."

Blushing, Bess slid her bags under the chair next to Nancy's and struggled out of her coat. George followed suit.

"Where have you guys been?" Nancy whispered when Regis turned to write on the chalkboard.

"We went to the *Herald* office, but the reporter we want is out until Monday," George whispered. "We would have come right back, but Bess"—she threw her cousin a freezing look—"decided she just *had* to do some shopping. I finally managed to drag her back here after she'd picked all the dress shops clean."

"No way!" Bess protested, leaning forward. "It just so happens that I needed a few—"

"Ms. Marvin," Regis barked, turning around from the chalkboard. "Would you like to share your story with the rest of the class?"

Bess sank down in her chair and shook her head. When Regis turned back to the board, Nancy and Bess exchanged glances and both stifled their giggles.

As the students continued with the lesson, Nancy glanced over her shoulder at Gloria, who was working in the aisle behind her. Nancy noticed that she didn't have her shoulder bag with her. Did that mean the files she had taken might be up in her room?

Seized by a sudden inspiration, Nancy whispered, "Bess, George, I'll be right back."

"But, Nan—" Bess protested.

While Regis was busy showing Paul how to cut up the sponge cake for the petit fours, Nancy slipped out of the classroom.

She rushed down the hall to Sophie's office. It was empty. "Oh, great," she moaned. "Now, how am I going to find out which room Gloria's in?"

Then her eyes fell on a notebook on Sophie's desk labeled Registration. Flipping through its pages, she found what she was looking for.

"Can I help you with something?"

Her heart pounding, Nancy closed the registration book casually. Looking up, she saw Baird standing just inside the door, his pale blue eyes flashing suspiciously.

"Oh, hi, Mr. Goldensen," Nancy said, smiling. "I was just looking for something to write on. I wanted to leave Sophie a note."

Baird raised his eyebrows. "I believe she's gone out for the afternoon."

"Oh," Nancy said. "I'll catch her later, then." Without waiting for Baird's response, she breezed by him and out the door.

"That was a close one," Nancy muttered to herself as she headed upstairs.

Gloria's bedroom was three doors down from the girls'. Luckily for Nancy, it was unlocked. Once inside, she wasted no time. She looked around, spotted a desk, and went over to it immediately.

On top of the desk was a portable computer and a large manila envelope. Nancy picked up the envelope eagerly and opened it. Inside were the files!

She pulled them out—and gasped. They were the same ones she and Bess had looked at on Wednesday, the ones marked "Recipes—Wolfe Culinary Institute Staff and Guest Chefs." She leafed through them quickly. There was Ham, Cheese, and Onion Pie, and Rhubarb-Apple Cobbler—

What was Gloria doing with these recipes?

Laying the files back on the desk, Nancy bent down. Then she switched on the portable computer. After punching a few buttons, she found the answer she was looking for.

Gloria had typed the institute's recipes into the computer and renamed them. Ham, Cheese, and Onion Pie had become Cheddar and Virginia Ham Pie. Rhubarb-Apple Cobbler was now Gloria's Apple-Rhubarb Treat.

Then Nancy found in the computer a letter from Gloria to her book publisher, with that day's date on it. The first line read: "Here is the latest batch of recipes for my new cookbook."

Nancy shut off the computer and straightened up

slowly. Gloria was stealing recipes from the institute's archives, hoping to boost her failing career.

Nancy heard the door click behind her. She spun around. Gloria stood in the doorway, her amber eyes blazing angrily. She glared at Nancy and warned, "You won't get away with this!"

13

A Punctured Alibi

Gloria slammed the door behind her and took a step toward Nancy.

"For once I'm glad I had a headache—if I hadn't come up for some aspirin, I never would have found you in here," Gloria spat out. "How dare you break into my room!"

Nancy crossed her arms defiantly and retorted, "And how dare *you* steal recipes from the institute and try to publish them as your own."

Gloria stopped in her tracks, her mouth hanging open. "How did you—" She glanced at the portable computer. "So you've been snooping around, haven't you, Ms. Hotshot Detective?" she snapped. "Well, guess what? It's my word against yours. And whom do you think people will believe—the famous writer or a teenager with an overactive imagination?"

"I think they'll believe me—when I show them this evidence," Nancy shot back. She picked up the manila envelope and held it firmly.

Gloria glared at her. Then her expression softened. "Don't do this to me," she begged, holding her hands out. "That bookstore clerk you talked to was right—my books haven't sold well these last few years. I'm just trying to make a living. I'm not doing anyone any harm—not really."

"You don't call blowing up ovens and poisoning people's salads doing harm?" Nancy replied, hoping to make Gloria confess something. "Or throwing knives, or—"

"What are you talking about?" Gloria cried out. "You think *I* did all that stuff?" She laughed bitterly. "You've got the wrong person, Nancy. I may have . . . borrowed a few recipes from the institute, but I'm not violent or crazy! I had nothing to do with the incidents that have been happening here."

Then Gloria dropped her gaze. "Although I—well, I guess I'd better tell you. I was the one who hit you on the head on Tuesday night, near the cellar door."

Nancy was startled. "Why?"

"I was in the office, looking through the files," Gloria explained. "I heard you out there, prowling around. I knew you were a detective, and I was afraid you'd catch me in the act—I had recipes spread out all over the place. I figured I'd just knock you down, grab the recipes, and run. But I'm afraid I hit you too hard."

"Thanks a lot," Nancy muttered. "What did you hit me with?"

"One of my cookbooks—*Gloria's Light Lunches*. I happened to be carrying it with me," Gloria replied. "It's one of my best," she added.

"I'm sure," Nancy said dryly. Then she lapsed into a brief silence, reviewing what she had just learned. Was Gloria telling the truth?

"Why should I believe you about not doing all those other things?" Nancy asked finally.

"Why would I volunteer the information about hitting you on the head, then lie about everything else?" Gloria retorted hotly. "I didn't have to confess to you. I mean, I could go to jail for assaulting you."

Nancy had to admit that she had a point. "Well, we're going down to Sophie's office right now and telling her the whole story," she insisted, waving the manila envelope. "You first," she said to Gloria, nodding at the door.

But when they got downstairs, they found that Sophie was still out.

Louis Drake passed them in the hall. "You're looking for Sophie?" he said, wiping his hands on his white apron. "I just talked to her on the phone. She's stuck out in Duck Landing—it's snowing, and the roads are getting bad. I think she's planning to spend the night there."

"Where's Duck Landing?" Nancy asked.

"About forty miles away," he replied. "Excuse me, I've got to see about dinner."

Gloria turned to Nancy. "Oh, well," she said with a relieved grin. "I guess this little talk with Sophie just wasn't meant to be."

"We'll postpone it until tomorrow," Nancy told her firmly. "Until then, stick around, okay?"

"If the roads are so bad, where am I going to go?" Gloria said, shrugging.

When Nancy got back to the girls' room, she found Bess and George there, sifting through Bess's shopping bags.

"Where did you rush off to, Nan?" George asked.

"Yeah, you missed a great class," Bess added. "We made a bunch of petit-whatchamacallits that looked like fuzzy dice, and gift-wrapped boxes—"

"—and then served them on mirrors and pieces of colored glass," George finished.

Nancy plopped into a chair. "Well, while you guys were making fuzzy dice, I was busy getting the goods on Gloria Chen." She proceeded to explain what had happened.

"Gloria caught you in her room?" Bess exclaimed, her blue eyes wide. "Nan, you could have been in terrible danger! After all she's done to you and everyone else here—"

"But don't you see?" Nancy cut in. "I don't think Gloria is X."

"If Gloria isn't X," George said slowly, "then who is?"

"That's what I *still* plan to find out," Nancy declared. She got up from her chair and walked over to a window. Louis Drake was right about the snow. It was blindingly white outside.

"I heard on the radio that this is going to be a really major blizzard," George remarked. "Twelve inches by midnight. And lots of high winds."

Bess had pulled the morning's *Putney Grove Herald* out of one of her shopping bags. "How dare that reporter take the weekend off," she muttered, tossing it on the bed. "We could have had the mystery solved by now."

Nancy walked over to the bed and picked the paper up. "I never did read this article from beginning to end. Maybe I should do that now."

"Help yourself," Bess said.

After a while, Nancy murmured, "This is interesting."

"What?" George called out from the bathroom. She and Bess had started changing for dinner.

"There's a small article right underneath the one about the institute," Nancy replied. "Did you guys happen to notice it?"

Bess came over to the bed and sat down next to Nancy.

"'Another Culinary Giant in Crisis,'" Bess read out loud. "What other culinary giant?"

"The Leblanc School in New York City," Nancy explained. "Remember Sophie telling us about it? She said it was one of her competitors."

George emerged from the bathroom. "So what's so interesting about this Leblanc article?"

Nancy held the paper up and read out loud:

NEW YORK—Renowned chef Bertrand Leblanc yesterday announced plans to close his thirty-year-old cooking school, the Leblanc School, citing declining enrollment as his primary reason.

Since the opening of the popular and innovative Wolfe Culinary Institute five years ago, the Leblanc and other cooking schools have seen their business slipping.

The institute's business manager, Paul Leblanc, Bertrand Leblanc's son, was on vacation and could not be reached for comment. The senior Leblanc's immediate plans include—

Then Nancy stopped reading and looked up. "Paul Leblanc!" she exclaimed. "Of course—Paul White! Don't you get it? Leblanc. The word *blanc* means 'white' in French."

"Paul Leblanc," George said thoughtfully. "You think our Paul might be this guy Bertrand Leblanc's son?"

128

Nancy nodded. "It fits, doesn't it?"

Bess lifted a hand. "Hold it. Let me get this straight. You're saying Paul Leblanc showed up here under an alias—for what reason?"

"This article says the Leblanc School's enrollment has been slipping since the Wolfe Culinary Institute opened," George offered. "Maybe Paul thought that trashing this place would help his father's business get back on its feet."

"That sounds like a good theory to me," Nancy said. "And it would explain a lot of his weird behavior." She shook her head. "I kept doubting Paul's guilt because he had an airtight alibi for the night I got hit on the head. But now we know Gloria was responsible for that."

"I don't know, Nan," Bess said doubtfully. "How can you be sure Paul's our culprit? Have you completely ruled out Gloria and Baird? And Lila?"

"Lila, yes," Nancy replied. "I'll explain about her later. But as for Gloria and Baird—" Then her eyes lit up. "I know—we'll set a trap. That way we'll be sure to get the right person. Bess, George, I'll need your help."

"Will it involve bees, skiing, or electrical outlets?" Bess moaned. "If so, count me out."

Nancy smiled. "None of the above. Now, listen closely—here's the plan. When we go down to dinner . . ."

14

Trapped in the Cellar

"My favorite meal was at a restaurant in Paris," Regis was saying to Lila and Teddy over the salad course. "A splendid shrimp dish with a hint of cayenne pepper, just enough to create a piquancy I'll never forget."

Nancy, sitting at the next table with Bess and Paul, leaned over to Paul and said, "Sounds good, doesn't it?"

"Hmm?" Paul was bent over his orange and arugula salad with a dark expression on his face.

"Mr. Brady was describing his favorite meal," Nancy explained. "What do you think yours would be, Paul?"

Paul scowled at her. "I don't have one."

Nancy turned to Bess. "How about you?"

"Me?" Bess giggled nervously. "I love my dad's tuna casserole. He does this special trick where he crumbles potato chips on top before putting it in the oven. And you know what I really love? Chocolate chip cookie dough. You know, before it's been cooked. . . ."

A long silence followed while the salad plates were cleared and the main course was served: pizzas topped with goat cheese, ham, and pineapple.

Nancy glanced over her shoulder. George was sitting at the table behind theirs with Baird and Gloria. Gloria looked more subdued than usual. She's probably thinking about having to face Sophie tomorrow, Nancy guessed.

Nancy turned back to her companions. "So did I tell you, Bess?" she said, raising her voice slightly. "I lost one of my gold heart-shaped earrings."

Bess gasped, right on cue. "You did? The ones your dad got you for Christmas?"

Nancy nodded. "Isn't that awful? I think it must have happened while I was looking for Truffles last night. I know I had both of them on during charades. But when we were getting ready for bed, I noticed that the left one was gone."

She watched Paul carefully. His eyes were on his plate, but he seemed to be listening.

"Nan?" George called over from her table. "Did I hear you say you lost one of your heart-shaped earrings?"

Nancy turned around. The plan was working smoothly—Baird and Gloria were listening, too.

"Isn't that awful, George?" Nancy replied.

"What are you going to do?" Bess piped up.

Nancy slid her chair back so she could address both tables at the same time. "I should probably look for it right away," she said, "since Monday is our last day here. I'm going to search the wine cellar tonight. When I found Truffles under the wine rack, he jumped up on me and started licking my face. He probably knocked the earring loose."

"Bess and I will help you," George volunteered.

Nancy shook her head. "No, really, it's not necessary. I can do it by myself." She glanced at her watch. "I want to make some phone calls after dinner, so I probably won't get to it until about eleven or so. And I know you guys—you'll be fast asleep by then."

"Thanks a lot," George said, grinning.

"You're welcome," Nancy teased, then returned to her dinner.

Taking a bite of her delicious pizza, Nancy thought excitedly about the trap she had just set. Now Paul, Gloria, and Baird all knew that she would be alone in the cellar. Would one of them take the bait and come after her?

By ten forty-five that night, the blizzard was at its peak. Seven inches of new snow had accumulated on the ground, and more continued to fall. Ferocious winds rattled the mansion's windows and whipped around the tree branches outside.

"How can anyone sleep through this racket?" Bess whispered as the girls crept through the dark upstairs hall.

George whispered to Nancy, "Nan, I think we should bag your plan. I just heard on the radio that they were closing the road into town due to icy conditions. If something should happen, the police won't be able to get here."

"I'll be fine," Nancy reassured her. "After all, you guys will be in the old office ready to provide backup at the first sign of trouble."

"I still don't like it," George grumbled.

"Maybe no one will show up," Nancy reminded her friends. "Although if Paul, Gloria, or Baird is really X, having a clear shot at me alone in the cellar will be too tempting to resist."

Nancy left Bess and George at their stakeout posts in the office and proceeded to the cellar. At the top of the stairs she flipped on a switch. A single bare bulb flickered on, casting a pale yellow glow over the room. Below were rows of wooden racks holding wine bottles.

There was just enough light to see but not very well. At the bottom of the stairs Nancy pulled her flashlight out and turned it on. Then she waited.

After a few minutes Nancy heard footsteps upstairs—or thought she did. The wind outside howled so fiercely, it was hard to be sure. Just in case, she positioned herself at the far side of the room, with her back turned to the stairs. She swung her flashlight in wide arcs, pretending to be engrossed in her search.

The cellar door opened. Someone started down the stairs.

Nancy waited, goose bumps prickling her skin. Who was it going to be? she wondered apprehensively.

"Did you find your earring, Ms. Drew?"

Nancy whirled around. Baird was standing at the foot of the stairs.

Nancy clicked off her flashlight. "Not yet," she replied slowly. "What brings you down here, Mr. Goldensen?"

Baird began walking toward her. Nancy tensed and instinctively took a step back. But when he reached her, he walked on past her.

Surprised, Nancy turned around. Baird was opening a circuit box on the wall. "The electricity went out in my room," he explained, flipping a switch. "This should take care of it."

He closed the circuit box and headed back for the stairs. "It's awfully lonely down here, isn't it?" he called over his shoulder. "Hope you don't scare easily. Good night."

When he'd left, Nancy glanced at the circuit box curiously. Baird hadn't tried to harm her. Did this mean he wasn't X? Or was he engaging in some sort of cat-and-mouse game with her?

The cellar door opened a crack. "Nan?" George called down softly. "Are you okay? We saw Baird."

"I'm fine, thanks," Nancy called back. "Nothing happened. You'd better get back to your post before anyone sees you."

Alone once more, Nancy flicked on her flashlight and began pacing. She checked her watch; it was a few minutes after eleven. Would anyone else show up? she wondered.

At eleven-fifteen her question was answered. Footsteps approached the cellar door. Moving quickly, she crouched down next to one of the wine racks and resumed her "search."

The door opened. Heart pounding and senses alert, Nancy cast her flashlight about, trying to look preoccupied.

She heard creaking stairs, then soft footsteps, then the sound of glass clinking. The footsteps came closer, and closer. . . .

Nancy leapt to her feet and spun around—and just in time. Paul White was standing a few feet away from her, clutching a wine bottle in his hand. Even in the dim light, she could see his green eyes blazing menacingly at her.

Nancy looked at him squarely. "So you're the one," she said. "Why don't you turn yourself in before it's too late?"

"Turn myself in?" Paul snapped. "Are you crazy?" His fingers tightened around the neck of the bottle.

"I know you were only trying to save your father's business," Nancy said quickly. She wanted to get him talking—anything to keep him from becoming violent.

Paul stared at her, surprised. "So you figured that out, did you?"

"I'm sure you didn't mean to do anyone any harm," Nancy added, forcing herself to smile sympathetically.

"That's right," Paul muttered. "Do you know what my original plan was? To come here and learn the institute's secrets so that I could go back and help get my dad's school back on its feet." He added bitterly, "I told him I was taking a week's vacation. I was going to surprise him."

"So what happened?" Nancy prompted.

"When I got here and saw how many enemies Regis Brady had, an idea came to me," Paul explained, his mouth curling into a cruel grin. "Why not pretend someone was after him—really stir up some trouble for the institute? That seemed like a better way to accomplish my mission.

"Then I started coming up with all kinds of ways to bring the place down," he went on, relishing his story. "I figured, at this rate the institute would be ruined fast, and the Leblanc School would rise to the top again."

He paused, gritting his teeth. "And I would have succeeded, except that he—that Dad—"

"Went ahead and closed his school, anyway?"

136

Nancy said gently. "When you read about his decision in this morning's paper, you were furious, weren't you?"

"I tried to talk him out of it," Paul rasped. "But he wouldn't listen to me. He's never listened to me!" A look of pain crossed his face. "He figured out years ago that I had no talent for cooking. From that moment on, I was a worthless good-for-nothing as far as he was concerned."

Nancy thought of how Paul could never do anything right in the dessert classes. It all made sense now.

Nancy tried to draw him out. "You entered one of your dad's recipes in the dessert contest, didn't you? And you took a post office box in New York, so he wouldn't find out."

Paul looked startled. Then he narrowed his eyes, as if sizing Nancy up.

"You're pretty smart," he murmured darkly. "A little too smart, if you ask me." He moved toward her slowly. "You're trying to make me believe you're on my side, but you're not. You can't wait to call the cops on me."

Nancy took a step backward, nervously eyeing the bottle in Paul's hand. "Of course I'm not—" she began.

Paul lunged at her with the bottle. Thinking quickly, Nancy pointed the beam of her flashlight right into his eyes.

Paul stumbled, blinded by the bright light. Nancy

used the opportunity to duck behind one of the wine racks.

But Paul recovered his vision quickly. "You're not getting out of here alive!" he growled, then hurled the bottle at her.

Nancy huddled behind the wine rack. She winced as the bottle crashed noisily against the wall behind her.

Through the holes in the wine rack, she could see Paul reach for another bottle to fling at her.

Nancy's mind raced frantically as she tried to come up with an escape plan. Paul stood between her and the stairs. Would Bess and George hear the commotion and come to her aid?

Suddenly the cellar was plunged into complete darkness!

15

Danger for Dessert

"Hey!" Paul cried out. "What's going on?"

Thinking fast, Nancy realized that they were having a blackout—probably as a result of the storm. This could be her opportunity to escape. With the darkness and the noise of the howling winds, she might be able to get to the cellar door before Paul noticed.

She snapped off her flashlight and rose quietly from behind the wine rack.

"Oh, I get it," Paul snarled. "The storm's zapped the electricity. Well, good—now we're really cut off from civilization."

Nancy used Paul's voice to judge her position. She took a few steps forward, then to the right, moving as silently as possible. She held her hands in front of her to feel for obstacles.

"Don't think I can't find you now," Paul warned.

Nancy froze for a moment. Then, when she realized that he must be bluffing, she continued, heart racing.

Nancy's foot found the bottom stair. She started up, slowly, testing for creaks on each stair before putting her full weight on it.

Careful as she was, Nancy's luck ran out. She finally hit the loudest spot on the creakiest stair, and not even the wind could obscure the noise completely.

She heard Paul start moving toward her, then the sound of more breaking glass. "You're not getting away from me!" he called out threateningly.

Nancy raced up the rest of the stairs. She reached the cellar door, flung it open, and broke into a run. As she passed the closed door of the old office, she wondered what had happened to Bess and George. Were they all right?

As she continued running down the pitch-black hallway, she began shouting, "Help!"

She could hear Paul catching up to her, his footsteps pounding on the floor of the corridor. When she reached the middle of the lobby, she felt his fingers clutch at her arm.

Nancy wrenched away, then cast a quick glance over her shoulder. Her eyes had adjusted to the darkness, and she could see Paul just a few feet behind her, raising his arm. In his hand was a jaggedly broken wine bottle!

"End of the line," Paul said menacingly.

The bottle swung down toward Nancy's head.

Nancy ducked just in time. She then delivered a swift karate kick to Paul's shin.

"Ow!" he cried out in pain.

Knowing he'd be off balance for a few short seconds, Nancy planned her next move. As far as she could tell in the darkness, she had her back to the front door. To get to the stairs or even the south wing, she'd have to get past Paul. Her best chance of escape was to head outside.

Nancy spun around, grabbed the front door handle, and pulled. A blast of frigid, snowy air blew in her face, stunning her.

"What do you think you're doing?" she heard Paul yell.

Gathering her courage, Nancy raced out into the knee-deep snow. But the piercing wind kept her from going very fast, and without a coat on, she froze almost instantly.

"Don't you know by now that I can outrun you?" she heard Paul shout from somewhere behind her.

Alarmed, Nancy tried to speed up. She had no idea where she was going—the snow was falling too thickly. All she could see was a muffling curtain of white.

Panting, she continued to run. She didn't know if she could keep it up for much longer, but she knew she had to try.

Without warning, the snow-covered ground fell away in front of her. Nancy stopped in her tracks just in time. She stood at the edge of a cliff. A hundred feet below churned the icy Hudson River.

Nancy turned swiftly, her nerves alert. Paul was right behind her. She tried to swerve around him, but he was too fast. He grabbed her arm, and the two of them struggled fiercely.

At last Nancy managed to knock the broken bottle out of Paul's hand. She heard it clatter down the cliffside and shatter on the rocks somewhere below.

Then Paul pushed her—hard.

"No!" Nancy shouted as she felt herself going over the edge.

Just in time, Nancy's bare hands managed to grab the snow-covered ledge. Clinging precariously to a rock, she dangled in the air. Her feet searched desperately for a toehold, but she found nothing.

"I guess this is goodbye," Paul said with a chuckle. Raising his boot, he prepared to crush her slipping fingers.

"Wait!" Nancy panted, stalling for time. "Don't you think that—"

But she was interrupted by the yipping sound of a dog's bark, suddenly near at hand. Then the yips turned into deep growling. Paul was yelling, "Get off me, you— Hey, my ankles!" Then he screamed in pain.

Taking a deep breath, Nancy gathered what little strength she had left and pulled herself up. She swung her legs over the ledge and scrambled to her feet.

Paul was rolling in the snow just a few feet away, trying to fight off Peaches and Truffles. The corgis had their jaws clamped down on both of his ankles and were pulling his legs this way and that.

Ignoring the pain in her hands, Nancy curled the right one into a tight fist. She leaned over and delivered a swift uppercut to Paul's jaw.

He sank back in the snow, stunned. As soon as he stopped moving, Peaches and Truffles let go and ran to Nancy, leaping up to lick her face and hands.

As she knelt, exhausted, in the snow, Nancy heard Bess, George, and Regis rushing toward her through the stormy darkness, calling out her name.

"This tastes great," Nancy said, cupping the mug of hot chocolate in her hands.

"Is the fire warm enough?" George asked. "I could throw on more logs—"

"It's fine, thanks," Nancy replied. She leaned back on the living room couch and adjusted the afghan around her legs. "Besides, I'm not the only one here who went trekking out in the storm. You guys must be chilled to the bone, too."

Bess and George looked at each other. "Well, *we* didn't go out without a coat," George remarked.

"Or a hat or gloves or boots," Bess continued. "I can't believe you did that, Nan."

"I didn't have much choice," Nancy told her. "What happened to you guys, anyway? You were supposed to be doing backup duty in that office."

"We blew it, Nan," George said apologetically. "Through the keyhole, we saw Paul go down to the cellar. We waited for a few minutes, but we didn't hear anything. We realized that maybe we were in over our heads. I went upstairs to wake some people, for extra backup. Bess stayed in the office, in case you had trouble."

"After George left, I heard all that glass breaking," Bess said, shuddering. "I realized you needed me, so I started looking around for some sort of weapon. But then the lights went out."

"Right," George said. "I was in the middle of waking Regis up when that happened. His room was the first one I came to."

"The blackout thing really scared me. I didn't know what to do," Bess explained ruefully. "Then, the next thing I knew, I heard you running past the office door and Paul shouting and you calling for help. I tried to follow you through the dark, but when I got to the lobby, the front door was open and you were outside."

"By that time, I'd gotten Regis up," George went

144

on. "He was furious when he found out Paul was the one who'd poisoned him. He volunteered his services—plus his dogs."

"Boy, did Truffles and Peaches ever come in handy," Nancy said, grinning. "Corgis are sheep-herding dogs—they instinctively nip ankles at the first sign of chaos."

"Phooey," Bess scoffed. "Those dogs were getting back at Paul for kidnapping Truffles."

"Speaking of which—remember Paul's so-called cold last night?" Nancy said. "It must have been an allergic reaction to Truffles, after Paul had lured him down to the cellar."

Bess smacked herself on the forehead. "That's right, he's allergic to dogs!"

Regis appeared in the doorway just then. Peaches and Truffles trotted at his heels.

"I've locked up Mr. White—or Leblanc, or whatever his name is—in his bathroom," he announced to the girls. "Teddy Angell and the Morris brothers are guarding him. The phone lines are down, so we can't call the police just yet. Maybe we can get through in the morning."

"Thanks for all your help, Mr. Brady," Nancy told him.

"I'm just glad you caught the rat, Ms. Drew," Regis replied crisply, then spun around on his feet. "Come along, Peaches, Truffles."

After he left, Bess said, "I'm so glad Nancy's

wrapped up this case." She sighed. "Now maybe I can concentrate on the reason we came to this place: desserts."

Nancy and George broke into laughter.

"No, I'm serious," Bess protested.

"We know," George replied, her brown eyes sparkling.

On Valentine's Day the main kitchen buzzed with activity. All the students and staff were gathered together to prepare for the big party.

Sophie, who was dressed in a red jumpsuit, waved her hand. "Listen up!" she called out. "Remember, each one of you is responsible for a dessert. The only requirement is that it be heart-shaped. The three contest winners—well, I guess only two of you are left now. Anyway, we'd like you to make your contest entries so they can be presented officially."

"You got it!" Teddy replied, and George nodded.

"I only have one other request," Sophie continued, turning to Alicia. "I wish you'd share your specialty with us. I don't think many people in this kitchen have had the pleasure of tasting your famous Mississippi Mud Pie."

"I'd be happy to," Alicia replied, beaming.

Regis, who was standing nearby, scowled deeply. "You know, Alicia, *my* Mississippi Mud Pie is the real thing. I defy anybody to come up with anything half as delectable."

146

Alicia smiled sweetly at him. "If you're so sure about that, why don't you put one together and we'll see?"

Regis narrowed his eyes. "I accept your challenge, madam." He turned briskly and pointed at two of the young assistant chefs, Gerard and Audrey. "You there, and you—fetch me my apron. And get me a bowl. No, not that one—"

Sophie stepped over to Nancy, George, and Bess. "Before you get busy, girls, I wanted to fill you in on the latest." She lowered her voice. "I heard from Officer Reed just a few minutes ago. Paul's father, Bertrand Leblanc, drove up here yesterday. He convinced Paul to confess to everything."

"Everything?" Bess echoed. "The flowers in the salad, the knife—"

"And Alicia's scarf?" Nancy interrupted. "Did he admit to stealing it from her and planting it in the hall, to make her look guilty?"

Sophie nodded. "He said he was trying to take advantage of the hostility between Regis and Alicia."

"Did he own up to the rest of it, too?" George asked. "The aerosol can in the oven, the icing on the wall, kidnapping Truffles—have I covered it all?"

"Don't forget the extension cord in our bathroom," Bess huffed. "And those bees!"

"Mr. Leblanc told Officer Reed that beekeeping was one of Paul's hobbies," Sophie explained. She added dryly, "For someone who doesn't know how to cook, Paul sure has a lot of other talents."

"He's definitely very clever," Nancy agreed. "He even thought to point out that there was something wrong with Regis's salad in Officer Reed's presence. And to come to my rescue after my skiing accident—"

"—just hours after he'd skied out there himself and hidden some bricks under the snow, in anticipation of Gloria's skiing party," Sophie finished.

"What did you decide to do about Gloria, by the way?" Bess asked.

Sophie sighed. "After Nancy told me what Gloria had done, I asked her to leave here immediately. I won't press charges, but if she ever tries to publish a cookbook again, I told her, I'll go public with her crimes."

Sophie laid her hand on Nancy's arm. "You've done so much," she said gratefully. "If it weren't for you, I'd be having a funeral for my school instead of this wonderful party." She broke into a grin. "And you did it all without me! I can't believe I was stranded in Duck Landing on the night you broke the case!"

"The night the three of us broke the case," Nancy corrected, smiling at Bess and George. "I couldn't have done it without my able assistants."

"Your *hungry* assistants," Bess said, rubbing her hands together. "Why don't we get started on these heart-shaped desserts?"

148

After Bess and George had gone off to find some utensils, Nancy leaned over to Sophie and said, "Where's Baird, by the way? I haven't seen him around."

Sophie sighed heavily. "I was going to tell you. I've asked him to leave the institute."

Nancy looked startled. "Really? Why?"

"I guess he wasn't the loyal employee I thought he was," Sophie explained. "I found out from a woman I know at the *Putney Grove Herald* that Baird was the source for that awful article."

"How terrible!" Nancy gasped.

"You were right about the conversation you overheard in my office, Nancy," Sophie continued sadly. "The *Herald* reporter was calling for me, and Baird happened to answer the phone. The guy apparently buttered up Baird, and he ended up telling the reporter a lot of nasty stuff."

"But why?" Nancy asked her.

"Baird told me yesterday when I confronted him," Sophie replied heavily. "He's never been happy working under me. So when things started going crazy here last week, he began to hope I'd crack under the strain and hand the reins over to him. A damaging article about the institute seemed like a good way to speed things up."

"This must really be upsetting for you," Nancy said sympathetically.

"Yes—and no." Sophie shrugged. "I'm looking

forward to finding someone new for the position—someone who'll really enjoy working for me."

"That's the spirit," Nancy said. "And what about Regis and Alicia? Have you decided which one to hire?"

Sophie shook her head. "I'm tempted to tell them they can share the job—provided they can learn to get along," she murmured. "But maybe I'm asking for the impossible . . ."

"Alicia, you're going to crawl into a hole when you taste my pie!" Regis's loud voice boomed from across the kitchen.

Alicia popped her head out of one of the spice cupboards. "You wish!" she replied.

Sophie and Nancy looked at each other, then broke into laughter.

By midafternoon all the desserts were finished and the party began in earnest. Everyone assembled in the dining hall, which had been transformed by pink streamers, red balloons, and fresh flowers from the greenhouse.

"My Raspberry Chiffon Cake came out beautifully, if I say so myself," George said proudly to Nancy and Bess.

"Well, my Valentine Triple-Chocolate Mousse Torte is nothing short of perfect, I must admit," Bess declared. "But what I want to know is, when do we get to taste all this stuff?"

Nancy laid her platter of heart-shaped strawberry tarts on the display table. "There's your answer,

Bess," she said, nodding toward the other end of the room.

Regis stood there, waving his arms majestically, his dogs beside him.

"Attention, ladies and gentlemen," Regis called out. "You are about to witness the presentation of the greatest Mississippi Mud Pie the world has ever tasted."

He turned to the doorway where Audrey, one of the assistant chefs, was standing with the pie in her hands. He nodded, and she entered nervously.

Everyone in the room watched as Audrey laid the pie on a table in front of Regis. He cut a small slice and tasted it.

"Magnificent!" he pronounced, beaming. "I invite you all to try it. You will agree that my pie possesses the most sublime flavors, the perfect marriage of chocolate and—"

Just then Gerard came running into the room. "Excuse me, Mr. Brady," he said breathlessly. "I'm sorry, sir. But there's been a mistake."

"Don't interrupt me, lad," Regis said grandly. "As I was saying, ladies and gentlemen, the perfect—"

"But you don't understand, sir," Gerard cut in. "I got the pies mixed up. I took Ms. Jones's out of the refrigerator by accident."

Regis dropped his fork. *"What?"*

"That's her pie, not yours," Gerard said in a voice barely above a whisper.

The room erupted into laughter as Regis turned beet red.

George elbowed Nancy. "There's your next job, Nan. 'The Case of the Mixed-up Pies.'"

"I've never been one to say no to a good mystery," Nancy replied, grinning happily.